stickfiguratively speaking

alice's adventures in wonderland

retold and illustrated
by Jamison Odone

PublishingWorks, Inc.
151 Epping Road
Exeter, NH 03833
603-778-9883

For Sales and Orders:
1-800-738-6603 or 603-772-7200

LCCN: 2009942221
ISBN-13: 978-1-935557-61-6

Alice's Adventures in Wonderland

retold and illustrated
by
Jamison Odone

this is new . . .

PW

PublishingWorks, Inc.
2010

CHAPTER ONE:
down the rabbit-hole

Alice was beginning to get very tired of sitting by her sister on the bank, and of having nothing to do; once or twice she had peeped into the book her sister was reading, but it had no pictures or conversations in it, "and what is the use of a book," thought Alice, "without pictures or conversations?"

Suddenly a white rabbit with pink eyes ran close by her.

She ran across the field after it, and was just in time to see it pop down a large rabbit-hole under the hedge. In another moment down went Alice after it, never once considering how in the world she was to get out again.

dumb dumb . . .

The rabbit-hole went straight on like a tunnel for some way, and then dipped suddenly down, so suddenly that Alice had not a moment to think about stopping herself before she found herself falling down what seemed to be a very deep well. Either the well was very deep, or she fell very slowly, for she had plenty of time as she went down to look about her, and to wonder what was going to happen next.

I miss my cat,
Dinah . . .

5

Down, down, down. Would the fall *never* come to an end? "I wonder how many miles I've fallen by this time?" she said aloud. "I must be getting somewhere near the centre of the earth. Let me see: that would be four thousand miles down, I think—I wonder if I shall fall right through the earth!"

I wonder what longitude and latitude I'm at?

Alice began to get rather sleepy, and went on saying to herself, in a dreamy sort of way, "Do cats eat bats? Do bats eat cats?" When suddenly,

THUMP!!

8

Alice was not a bit hurt, and she jumped up on to her feet in a moment. She looked up, but it was all dark overhead; before her was another long passage, and the White Rabbit was still in sight, hurrying down it. There was not a moment to be lost; away went Alice like the wind.

Oh my ears and whiskers how late it's getting.

She found herself in a long, low hall, which was lit up by a row of lamps hanging from the roof. There were doors all round the hall, but they were all locked. Suddenly she came upon a little three-legged table, all made of solid glass: there was nothing on it but a tiny golden key.

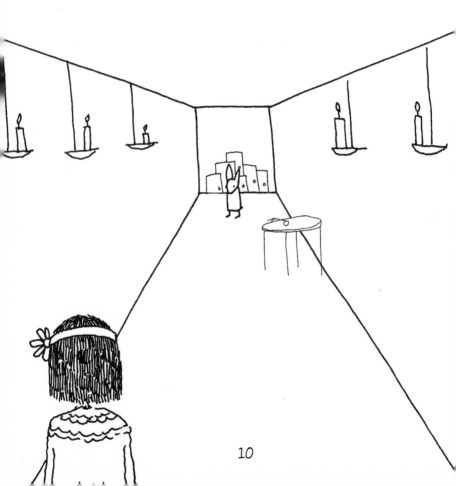

But, alas! Either the locks were too large, or the key was too small. She came upon a little door about fifteen inches high; she tried the little golden key in the lock, and to her great delight it fitted!

She knelt down and looked along the passage
into the loveliest garden you ever saw.

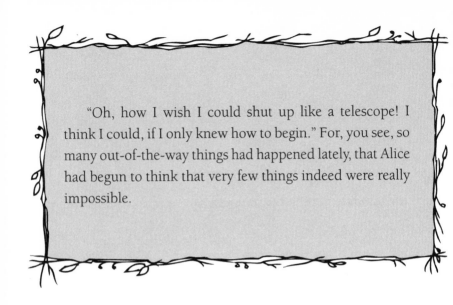

"Oh, how I wish I could shut up like a telescope! I think I could, if I only knew how to begin." For, you see, so many out-of-the-way things had happened lately, that Alice had begun to think that very few things indeed were really impossible.

There seemed to be no use in waiting by the little door; so she went back to the table. This time she found a little bottle on it which certainly was not there before.

hope this is not poison . . .

DRINK ME

. . . She very soon finished it off.

"What a curious feeling!" said Alice; "I must be shutting up like a telescope!" And so it was indeed; she was now only ten inches high, but, alas for poor Alice! when she got to the door, she found she had forgotten the little golden key, and when she went back to the table for it, she found she could not possibly reach it.

typical.

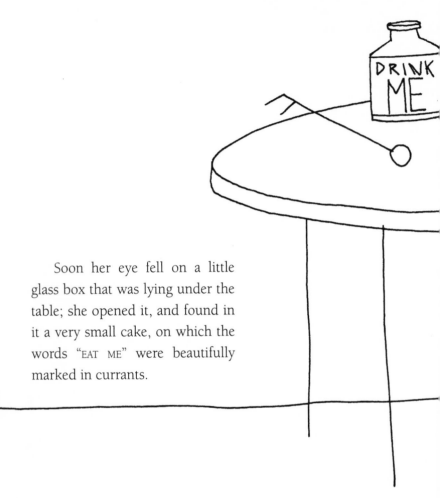

Soon her eye fell on a little glass box that was lying under the table; she opened it, and found in it a very small cake, on which the words "EAT ME" were beautifully marked in currants.

nums!

CHAPTER TWO:
the pool of tears

"Curiouser and curiouser," cried Alice (she was so much surprised, that for the moment she quite forgot how to speak good English); "now I'm opening out like the largest telescope that ever was!"

Just at this moment her head struck against the roof of the hall; in fact, she was now rather more than nine feet high, and she at once took up the little golden key and hurried off to the garden door.

goodbye feet . . .

Oh my poor, little feet,
I wonder who will put
on your shoes and
stockings now, dears?

18

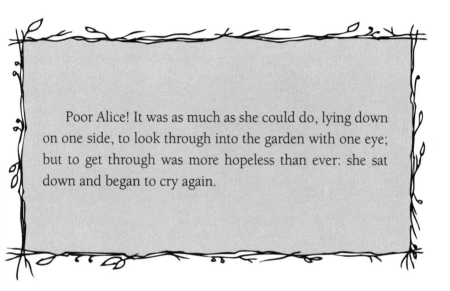

Poor Alice! It was as much as she could do, lying down on one side, to look through into the garden with one eye; but to get through was more hopeless than ever: she sat down and began to cry again.

"You ought to be ashamed of yourself," said Alice, "a great girl like you" (she might well say this), "to go on crying in this way! Stop, this moment, I tell you." But she went on all the same, shedding gallons of tears, until there was a large pool all round her, about four inches deep, and reaching half down the hall.

After a time she heard a little pattering of feet in the distance, and she hastily dried her eyes to see what was coming. It was the White Rabbit returning, splendidly dressed, with a pair of white kid gloves in one hand and a large fan in the other.

Oh the Duchess, the Duchess! Oh! Won't she be savage if I've kept her waiting!

Alice felt so desperate that she was ready to ask help of any one; so, when the Rabbit came near her, she began, in a low, timid voice,

If you please, Sir.

ahhhh!!

The Rabbit dropped the white kid gloves and the fan, and skurried away into the darkness.

Alice took up the fan and gloves, and, as the hall was very hot, she kept fanning herself all the time she went on talking.

How doth the little crocodile
Improve his shining tail,
And pour the waters of the Nile
On every golden scale!

How cheerfully he seems to grin,
How neatly spreads his claws,
And welcomes little fishes in
With gently smiling jaws!

"I'm sure those are not the right words," said poor Alice, and her eyes filled with tears again.

As she said this, she looked down at her hands, and was surprised to see that she had put on one of the Rabbit's little white kid gloves while she was talking. "How *can* I have done that?" she thought. "I must be growing small again."

. . . She was now about two feet high, and was going on shrinking rapidly; she soon found out that the cause of this was the fan she was holding, and she dropped it hastily, just in time to save herself from shrinking away altogether.

"That *was* a narrow escape!" said Alice, a good deal frightened at the sudden change, but very glad to find herself still in existence. "And now for the garden!"

As she said these words her foot slipped, and in another moment, splash! she was up to her chin in salt water.

I think these are my tears . . .

"I wish I hadn't cried so much!" said Alice as she swam about, trying to find her way out. "I shall be punished for it now, I suppose, by being drowned in my own tears!" It was high time to go, for the pool was getting quite crowded with the birds and animals that had fallen into it: there was a Duck and a Dodo, a Lory and an Eaglet, and several other curious creatures. Alice led the way, and the whole party swam to the shore.

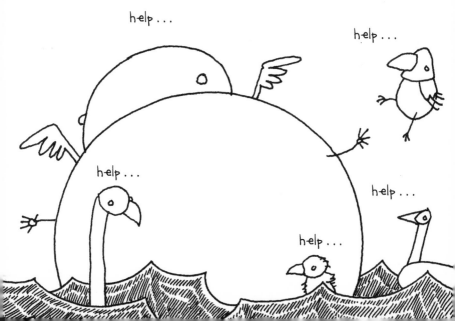

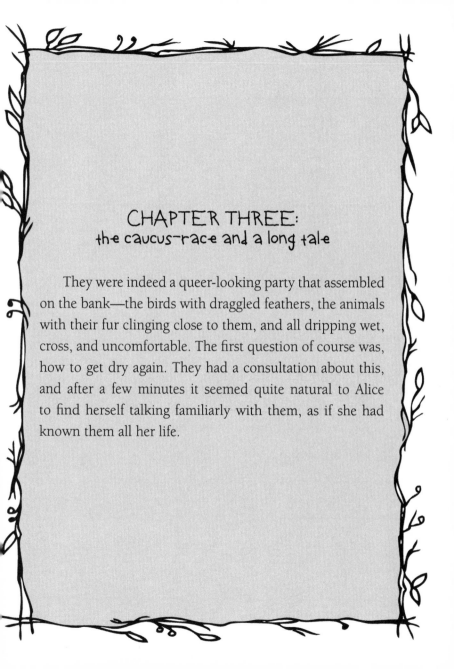

CHAPTER THREE:
the caucus-race and a long tale

They were indeed a queer-looking party that assembled on the bank—the birds with draggled feathers, the animals with their fur clinging close to them, and all dripping wet, cross, and uncomfortable. The first question of course was, how to get dry again. They had a consultation about this, and after a few minutes it seemed quite natural to Alice to find herself talking familiarly with them, as if she had known them all her life.

At last the Mouse, who seemed to be a person of some authority among them, called out, "Sit down, all of you, and listen to me! *I'll* soon make you dry enough!"

Mouse knows how to get us all dry.

William the Conqueror, whose cause was favoured by the pope, was soon submitted to by the English, who wanted leaders, and had been of late much accustomed to usurpation and conquest. Edwin and Morcar, the earls of Mercia and Northumbria, declared for him; and even Stigand, the patriotic archbishop of Canterbury, found it advisable ...
ARE YOU DRY YET!?!

"What I was going to say," said the Dodo, "was that the best thing to get us dry would be a caucus-race."

A CAUCUS-RACE!!!

RUN IN CIRCLES!
RUN IN CIRCLES!
RUN IN CIRCLES!
STOP!!

baby eagle
go run . .

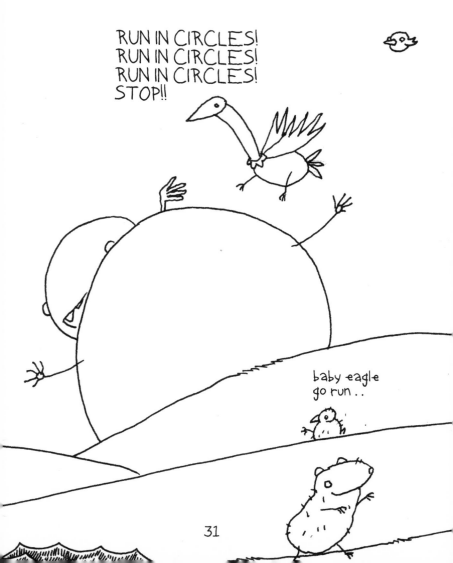

When they had been running half an hour or so, and were quite dry again, the Dodo suddenly called out, "The race is over!"

who won?

who won?

baby eagle go stop . . .

EVERYBODY WON! PRIZES FOR ALL!

"But who is to give the prizes?" quite a chorus of voices asked.

"Why, *she*, of course," said the Dodo, pointing to Alice with one finger; and the whole party at once crowded round her, calling out in a confused way, "Prizes, prizes!" Alice had no idea what to do, and in despair she put her hand into her pocket, and pulled out a box of comfits (luckily the salt water had not got into it), and handed them round as prizes. There was exactly one a-piece all round.

They sat down again in a ring, and begged the Mouse to tell them something more.

"You promised to tell me your history, you know," said Alice, "and why it is you hate—C and D," she added in a whisper, half afraid that it would be offended.

What's C and D?

Cats and dogs, of course!

Mine is a long, sad tale.

Fury said to a 
mouse, That he
met in the house,
"Let us both
go to law:
I will prosecute
you.—Come,
I'll take no
denial: We
must have a
trial; For
really this
morning I've
nothing to do."
Said the mouse
to the cur, "Such
a trial, dear sir,
With no jury
or judge,
would be
wasting
our
breath."
"I'll be
judge, I'll
be jury,"
Said cunning
old Fury:
"I'll try the
whole
cause,
and
condemn
you
to
death."

"You are not attending!" said the Mouse to Alice severely. "You insult me!" cried the Mouse, getting up and walking away.

"I didn't mean it!" pleaded poor Alice. "But you're so easily offended, you know." The Mouse only growled in reply. "Please come back, and finish your story!" Alice called after it; and the others all joined in chorus, "Yes, please do!" But the Mouse only shook its head impatiently, and walked a little quicker.

I wish Dinah were here. She'd be able to get him back.

Who's Dinah?

36

"Dinah's our cat. And she's such a capital one for catching mice, you can't think! And oh, I wish you could see her after the birds! Why, she'll eat a little bird as soon as look at it!" This speech caused a remarkable sensation among the party.

SHE'S THE
BEST CAT IN
THE WORLD!

On various pretexts they all moved off, and Alice was soon left alone. In a little while, however, she again heard a little pattering of footsteps in the distance.

CHAPTER FOUR:
the rabbit sends in a little bill

It was the White Rabbit, trotting slowly back again, and looking anxiously about as it went, as if it had lost something. Alice guessed in a moment that it was looking for the fan and the pair of white kid gloves, and she very good-naturedly began hunting about for them; but they were nowhere to be seen—everything seemed to have changed since her swim in the pool, and the great hall, with the glass table and the little door, had vanished completely.

The Duchess! The Duchess! Oh, my dear paws! Oh, my fur and whiskers! She'll get me executed as sure as ferrets are ferrets! Where can I have dropped them I wonder?

Why, Mary Ann, what are you doing out here? Run home this moment, and fetch me a pair of gloves and a fan! Quick, now!   NOW!

You got kinda bossy!

"He took me for his housemaid," she said to herself as she ran. "How surprised he'll be when he finds out who I am! But I'd better take him his fan and gloves—that is, if I can find them."

She came upon a neat little house, on the door of which was a bright brass plate, with the name "W. Rabbit" engraved upon it.

She went in without knocking, and hurried upstairs, in great fear lest she should meet the real Mary Ann, and be turned out of the house before she had found the fan and gloves.

She took up the fan and a pair of the gloves, and was just going to leave the room, when her eye fell upon a little bottle that stood near the looking-glass. There was no label this time with the words "DRINK ME"; but nevertheless she uncorked it, and put it to her lips.

I know *something* interesting is sure to happen if I drink this. So I'll just taste it . . . see what it does. I hope it will make me large again, for I'm quite tired of being such a little thing.

that's
quite
enough!

Before she had drunk half the bottle, she found her head pressing hard against the ceiling, and had to stoop to save her neck from being broken.

44

I almost wish I had never gone down the rabbit's hole. There should be a book written about this place.

She went on growing and growing, and, as a last resource, she put one arm out of the window, and one foot up the chimney.

Then came a little pattering of feet on the stairs. Alice knew it was the Rabbit coming to look for her; and she trembled till she shook the house, quite forgetting that she was now about a thousand times as large as the Rabbit, and had no reason to be afraid of it. Presently the Rabbit came up to the door, and tried to open it; but as the door opened inward, and Alice's elbow was pressed hard against it, that attempt proved a failure. Alice heard it say to itself, "Then I'll go round and get in at the window."

"*That* you won't!" thought Alice; and, after waiting till she fancied she heard the Rabbit just under the window, she suddenly spread out her hand, and made a snatch in the air. She did not get hold of anything, but she heard a little shriek and a fall.

She waited for some time without hearing anything more. At last came a rumbling of little cart-wheels, and the sound of a good many voices all talking together; she made out the words, "Where's the other ladder?—Here, Bill! The master says you've got to go down the chimney!"

"Oh, so Bill's got to come down the chimney, has he?" said Alice to herself. "I wouldn't be in Bill's place for a good deal; this fireplace is narrow, to be sure, but I *think* I can kick a little."

well . . . he shouldn't have
come down the chimney.

There
goes Bill!

There was a dead silence instantly; and Alice thought to herself, "I wonder what they *will* do next!" But she had not long to doubt, for the next moment a shower of little pebbles came rattling in at the window, and some of them hit her in the face. Alice noticed with some surprise that the pebbles were all turning into little cakes as they lay on the floor, and a bright idea came into her head. "If I eat one of these cakes," she thought, "it's sure to make some change in my size; and as it can't possibly make me larger, it must make me smaller, I suppose."

So she swallowed one of the cakes, and was delighted to find that she began shrinking directly.

As soon as she was small enough to get through the door, she ran out of the house, and found quite a crowd of little animals and birds waiting outside. They all made a rush at Alice the moment she appeared; but she ran off as hard as she could, and soon found herself safe in a thick wood.

I should eat you . . .

be careful!

don't trip.

"The first thing I've got to do," said Alice to herself, as she wandered about in the wood, "is to grow to my right size again; and the second thing is to find my way into that lovely garden. I think that will be the best plan." While she was peering about anxiously among the trees, a little sharp bark just over her head made her look up in a great hurry.

An enormous puppy was looking down at her! Hardly knowing what she did, she picked up a little bit of stick, and held it out to the puppy; then the puppy began a series of short charges at the stick, running a very little way forward each time and a long way back, and barking hoarsely all the while, till at last it sat down a good way off, panting, with its tongue hanging out of its mouth, and its great eyes half shut.

not me.

Hah! I prefer cats, myself.

This seemed to Alice a good opportunity for making her escape; so she set off at once, and ran till she was quite tired and out of breath, and till the puppy's bark sounded quite faint in the distance. "Oh dear! I'd nearly forgotten that I've got to grow up again. Let me see—how *is* it to be managed?"

I really have to get myself bigger. I suppose I ought to eat or drink something or other; but the great question is, what?

There was a large mushroom growing near her, about the same height as herself. She stretched herself up on tiptoe, and peeped over the edge of the mushroom; and her eyes immediately met those of a large blue caterpillar that was sitting on the top with its arms folded.

CHAPTER FIVE:
advice from a caterpillar

The Caterpillar and Alice looked at each other (for some time) in silence. At last the Caterpillar addressed her in a languid, sleepy voice. "Who are *you*?" said the Caterpillar.

Alice replied rather shyly, "I—I hardly know, sir, just at present—at least, I know who I *was* when I got up this morning, but I think I must have been changed several times since then."

"What do you mean by that?" said the Caterpillar, sternly. "Explain yourself."

"I cannot explain *myself*, I'm afraid, sir," said Alice, "because I'm not myself, you see."

"I don't see," said the Caterpillar.

Alice felt a little irritated at the Caterpillar's making such *very* short remarks, and she drew herself up and said, very gravely, "I think you ought to tell me who *you* are, first."

"Why?" said the Caterpillar.

Here was another puzzling question; and, as Alice could not think of any good reason, and as the Caterpillar seemed to be in a *very* unpleasant state of mind, she turned away.

"Come back!" the Caterpillar called after her. "I've something important to say!"

'You are old, Father William,' the young man said,
'And your hair has become very white;
And yet you incessantly stand on your head—
Do you think, at your age, it is right?'

'In my youth,' Father William replied to his son,
'I feared it might injure the brain;
But, now that I'm perfectly sure I have none,
Why, I do it again and again.'

'You are old,' said the youth, 'as I mentioned before,
And have grown most uncommonly fat;
Yet you turned a back-somersault in at the door—
Pray, what is the reason of that?'

'In my youth,' said the sage, as he shook his gray locks,
'I kept all my limbs very supple
By the use of this ointment—one shilling the box—
Allow me to sell you a couple.'

'You are old,' said the youth, 'and your jaws are too weak
For anything tougher than suet;
Yet you finish the goose, with the bones and the beak:
Pray, how did you manage to do it?'

'In my youth,' said his father, 'I took to the law,
And argued each case with my wife;
And the muscular strength, which it gave to my jaw,
Has lasted the rest of my life.'

64

'You are old,' said the youth; 'one would hardly suppose
That your eye was as steady as ever;
Yet you balance an eel on the end of your nose—
What made you so awfully clever?'

'I have answered three questions, and that is enough,'
Said his father; 'don't give yourself airs;
Do you think I can listen all day to such stuff?
Be off, or I'll kick you down stairs!'

That was wrong from beginning to end! What size is it that you wish to be anyway?

I just don't know!

"Well, I should like to be a *little* larger, sir, if you wouldn't mind," said Alice: "three inches is such a wretched height to be."

"It is a very good height indeed!" said the Caterpillar angrily, rearing itself upright as it spoke (it was exactly three inches high).

One side will make you grow taller and the other side will make you grow shorter...

"One side of *what*? The other side of *what*?" thought Alice to herself.

"Of the mushroom," said the Caterpillar, just as if she had asked it aloud; and in another moment it was out of sight. Alice remained looking thoughtfully at the mushroom for a minute, trying to make out which were the two sides of it; and, as it was perfectly round, she found this a very difficult question. However, at last she stretched her arms round it as far as they would go, and broke off a bit of the edge with each hand.

"And now which is which?" she said to herself, and nibbled a little of the right-hand bit to try the effect: the next moment she felt a violent blow underneath her chin; it had struck her foot! She was a good deal frightened by this very sudden change, as she was shrinking rapidly; so she set to work at once to eat some of the other bit.

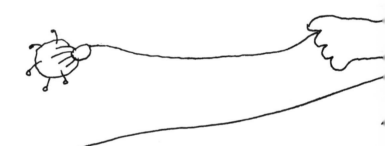

In another moment, she found that her shoulders were nowhere to be found; all she could see, when she looked down, was an immense length of neck. As there seemed to be no chance of getting her hands up to her head, she tried to get her head down to them, and was delighted to find that her neck would bend about easily in any direction, like a serpent.

I've seen a good many little girls in my time, but never one with such a neck as that. Always trying to eat my eggs!

I have tasted eggs certainly, but little girls eat eggs quite as much as serpents do, you know.

Alice crouched down among the trees as well as she could, for her neck kept getting entangled among the branches, and every now and then she had to stop and untwist it. After a while she remembered that she still held the pieces of mushroom in her hands, and she set to work very carefully, nibbling first at one and then at the other, and growing sometimes taller, and sometimes shorter, until she had succeeded in bringing herself down to her usual height. It was so long since she had been anything near the right size, that it felt quite strange at first; but she got used to it in a few minutes, and began talking to herself, as usual . . .

71

Come, there's half my plan done now! How puzzling all these changes are! I'm never sure what I'm going to be, from one minute to another! However, I've got back to my right size; the next thing is, to get into that beautiful garden—how is that to be done, I wonder?

As she said this, she came suddenly upon an open place, with a little house in it about four feet high. "Whoever lives there," thought Alice, "it'll never do to come upon them *this* size; why, I should frighten them out of their wits!" So she began nibbling at the right-hand bit again, and did not venture to go near the house till she had brought herself down to nine inches high.

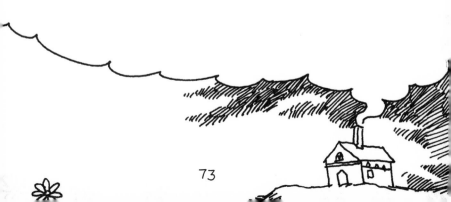

CHAPTER SIX:
pig and pepper

For a minute or two she stood looking at the house, and wondering what to do next, when suddenly a footman in livery came running out of the wood—(she considered him to be a footman because he was in livery; otherwise, judging by his face only, she would have called him a fish)—and rapped loudly at the door with his knuckles. It was opened by another footman in livery, with a round face, and large eyes like a frog; and both footmen, Alice noticed, had powdered hair that curled all over their heads. She felt very curious to know what it was all about, and crept a little way out of the wood to listen.

For the Duchess.
An invitation from the
Queen to play croquet.

From the Queen.
An invitation for the
Duchess to play croquet.

Then they both bowed low, and their curls got entangled together. Alice laughed so much at this, that she had to run back into
the wood for fear of their hearing her.

When she next peeped out, the Fish-Footman was gone, and the other was sitting on the ground near the door, staring stupidly up into the sky.

Alice went timidly up to the door, and knocked.

There's no use knocking, and that's for two reasons...

"First, because I'm on the same side of the door as you are; secondly, because they're making such a noise inside, no one could possibly hear you." And certainly there *was* a most extraordinary noise going on within—a constant howling and sneezing, and every now and then a great crash, as if a dish or kettle had been broken to pieces.

More like, there's no use talking to you. You're perfectly idiotic!

She opened the door and went in. The door led right into a large kitchen, which was full of smoke from one end to the other; the Duchess was sitting on a three-legged stool in the middle, nursing a baby; the cook was leaning over the fire, stirring a large cauldron which seemed to be full of soup.

"There's certainly too much pepper in that soup!" Alice said to herself, as well as she could for sneezing. There was certainly too much of it in the air. Even the Duchess sneezed occasionally; and as for the baby, it was sneezing and howling alternately without a moment's pause.

ACHOOOO!

ACHOOOO!

ACHOOOOO AND
HOWWWWWWWL!

81

The only two creatures in the kitchen that did not sneeze, were the cook, and a large cat, which was lying on the hearth and grinning from ear to ear.

I didn't know Cheshire
Cats grinned. In fact,
I didn't know cats could
grin. Hey, why did you
call me a pig?

You don't know much,
and that's a fact.
But I didn't call you
a pig-I was referring to
the baby . . . PIG!

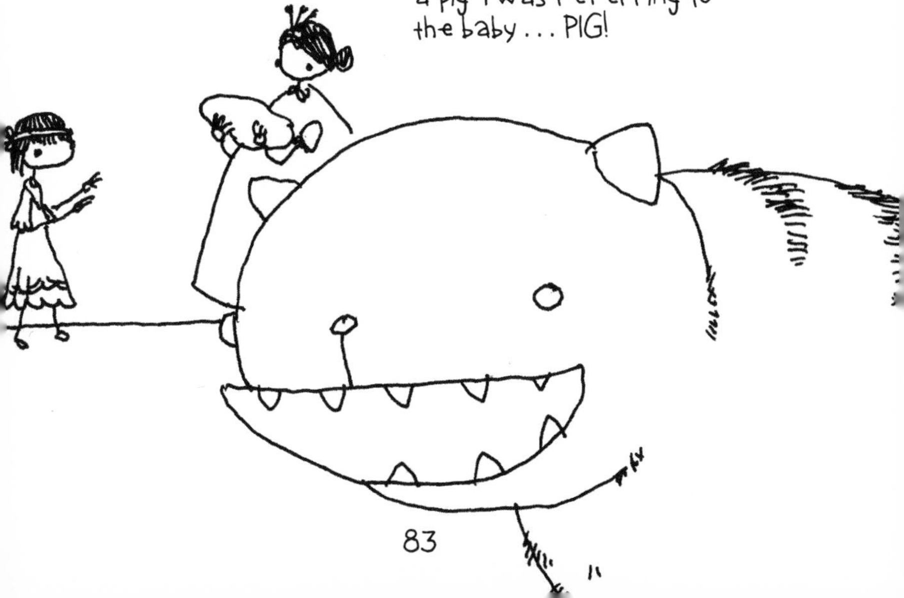

The cook took the cauldron of soup off the fire, and at once set to work throwing everything within her reach at the Duchess and the baby—the fire-irons came first; then followed a shower of saucepans, plates, and dishes. The Duchess took no notice of them even when they hit her; and the baby was howling so much already, that it was quite impossible to say whether the blows hurt it or not.

I HATE THAT PIG!
SHUT HIM UP OR I'LL
COOK HIM UP!

The Duchess began nursing her child again, singing a sort of lullaby to it as she did so, and giving it a violent shake at the end of every line:—

Speak roughly to your little boy,
And beat him when he sneezes
He only does it to annoy,
Because he knows it teases!

WOW! WOW! WOW!

I speak roughly to my boy
I beat him when he sneezes,
For he can thoroughly enjoy
The pepper when he pleases!

WOW! WOW! WOW!

"Here! You may nurse it a bit, if you like!" said the Duchess to Alice, flinging the baby at her as she spoke. "I must go and get ready to play croquet with the Queen." Alice caught the baby with some difficulty, as it was a queer-shaped little creature, and held out its arms and legs in all directions. As soon as she had made out the proper way of nursing it (which was to twist it up into a sort of knot, and then keep tight hold of its right ear and left foot, so as to prevent its undoing itself), she carried it out into the open air.

hoooowwwwlll . . .

If I don't take this child away with me, they're sure to kill him in a day or two. Wouldn't it be murder to leave him behind?

So she set the little creature down, and felt quite relieved to see it trot away quietly into the wood.

She was a little startled by seeing the Cheshire Cat sitting on a bough of a tree a few yards off.

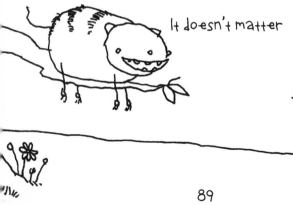

Cheshire Puss!
Would you tell me please
which way I ought to go
from here?

It doesn't matter

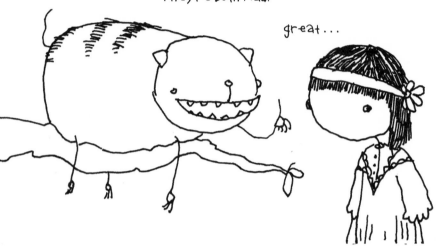

To the right lives a Hatter.
To the left lives a March Hare.
They're both mad!

great...

"But I don't want to go among mad people," Alice remarked.

"Oh, you can't help that," said the Cat; "we're all mad here. I'm mad. You're mad."

"How do you know I'm mad?" said Alice.

"You must be," said the Cat, "or you wouldn't have come here."

The Cat vanished. Alice was not much surprised at this, she was getting so well used to queer things happening. While she was still looking at the place where it had been, it suddenly appeared again. "By-the-bye, what became of the baby?" said the Cat. "I'd nearly forgotten to ask."

"It turned into a pig," Alice answered very quietly, just as if the Cat had come back in a natural way.

"I thought it would," said the Cat, and vanished again.

whoa!

Alice waited a little, half expecting to see it again, but it did not appear, and after a minute or two she walked on in the direction in which the March Hare was said to live. She looked up, and there was the Cat again, sitting on a branch of a tree. "Did you say 'pig,' or 'fig'?" said the Cat.

"I said 'pig,'" replied Alice.

"All right," said the Cat; and this time it vanished quite slowly, beginning with the end of the tail, and ending with the grin, which remained some time after the rest of it had gone.

I wish you wouldn't keep appearing and vanishing so suddenly; you make one quite giddy.

...get over it Al...

Well I've often seen a cat without a grin, but a grin without a cat! That's the most curious thing I ever saw in all my life.

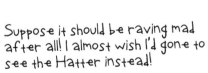

She had not gone much farther before she came in sight of the house of the March Hare. It was so large a house, that she did not like to go nearer till she had nibbled some more of the left-hand bit of mushroom, and raised herself to about two feet high.

Suppose it should be raving mad after all! I almost wish I'd gone to see the Hatter instead!

94

CHAPTER SEVEN:
a mad tea-party

There was a table set out under a tree in front of the house, and the March Hare and the Hatter were having tea at it. A Dormouse was sitting between them, fast asleep, and the other two were using it as a cushion, resting their elbows on it, and talking over its head. The table was a large one, but the three were all crowded together at one corner of it.

There's plenty of room. the
two of you are not very
welcoming of guests!

The Hatter had been looking at Alice for some time with great curiosity.

Why is a raven like a writing-desk?

"Come, we shall have some fun now!" thought Alice. "I'm glad they've begun asking riddles—I believe I can guess that," she added aloud. Alice thought over all she could remember about ravens and writing-desks, which wasn't much.

The Hatter had taken his watch out of his pocket, and was looking at it uneasily, shaking it every now and then, and holding it to his ear. "Two days wrong!" sighed the Hatter. "I told you butter wouldn't suit the works!" he added, looking angrily at the March Hare, "you shouldn't have put it in with the bread-knife."

The March Hare took the watch and looked at it gloomily; then he dipped it into his cup of tea, and looked at it again.

Alice had been looking over his shoulder with some curiosity.

"What a funny watch!" she remarked. "It tells the day of the month, and doesn't tell what o'clock it is!"

102

"If you knew Time as well as I do," said the Hatter, "you wouldn't talk about wasting *it*. It's *him*."

"I don't know what you mean," said Alice.

"Of course you don't!" the Hatter said, tossing his head contemptuously. "I dare say you never even spoke to Time!"

"Perhaps not," Alice cautiously replied; "but I know I have to beat time when I learn music."

"Ah! That accounts for it," said the Hatter. "He won't stand beating."

I know everything about time! I know Time, himself! I had to keep time while I sang a song at the great concert given by the Queen of Hearts!

Twinkle, twinkle little bat!
How I wonder where you're at!
Up above the world you fly
like a tea-tray in the sky!

zzzz ... twinkle twinkle

"Well, I'd hardly finished the first verse," said the Hatter, "when the Queen bawled out 'He's murdering the time! Off with his head!'"

"How dreadfully savage!" exclaimed Alice.

"And ever since that," the Hatter went on in a mournful tone, "he won't do a thing I ask! It's always six o'clock now."

Suppose we change the subject, I'm getting tired of this. I vote the young lady tells us a story.

"I'm afraid I don't know one," said Alice, rather alarmed at the proposal.

"Then the Dormouse shall!" they both cried. "Wake up, Dormouse!" And they pinched it on both sides at once.

Once upon a time there were three sisters...

I have a question about your story.

The Dormouse sulkily remarked, "If you can't be civil, you'd better finish the story for yourself."

This piece of rudeness was more than Alice could bear; she got up in great disgust, and walked off. The last time she saw them, they were trying to put the Dormouse into the teapot.

I'll never go there again!

"It's the stupidest tea-party I was ever at in all my life!"

Just as she said this she noticed that one of the trees had a door leading right into it. "That's very curious!" she thought. "But everything's curious to-day. I think I may as well go in at once." And in she went.

typical . . .

Once more she found herself in the long hall, and close to the little glass table. "Now, I'll manage better this time," she said to herself, and began by taking the little golden key, and unlocking the door that led into the garden. Then she set to work nibbling at the mushroom (she had kept a piece of it in her pocket) till she was about a foot high; then she walked down the little passage.

Table, key, doors!

this place—
I could get
used to!

She found herself at last in the beautiful garden, among the bright flower-beds and the cool fountains.

CHAPTER EIGHT:
the queen's croquet-ground

A large rose-tree stood near the entrance of the garden; the roses growing on it were white, but there were three gardeners at it, busily painting them red. Alice thought this a very curious thing, and she went nearer to watch them.

Seven flung down the brush, and had just begun, "Well of all the unjust things!" When his eye chanced to fall upon Alice, as she stood watching them, and he checked himself suddenly; the others looked round also, and all of them bowed low. "Would you tell me, please," said Alice, a little timidly, "why you are painting those roses?"

Five and Seven said nothing, but looked at Two. Two began, in a low voice, "Why, the fact is, you see, Miss, this here ought to have been a *red* rose-tree, and we put a white one in by mistake; and if the Queen was to find it out, we should all have our heads cut off, you know."

THE QUEEN! THE QUEEN!

There was a sound of many footsteps, and Alice looked round, eager to see the Queen. First came ten soldiers carrying clubs; these were all shaped like the three gardeners, oblong and flat, with their hands and feet at the corners; next the ten courtiers; these were ornamented all over with diamonds, and walked two and two, as the soldiers did. After these came the royal children; there were ten of them, and the little dears were all ornamented with hearts. Next came the guests, mostly Kings and Queens, and among them Alice recognized the White Rabbit. Last of all this grand procession, came THE KING AND QUEEN OF HEARTS.

When the procession came opposite to Alice, they all stopped and looked at her.

What's your name child? And who are these men painting the roses?

My name is Alice, your Majesty. How should I know who these men are . . . it's no business of mine.

The Queen turned crimson with fury, and, after glaring at her for a moment like a wild beast, began screaming,

"Come on, then!" roared the Queen, and Alice joined the procession, wondering very much what would happen next.

"It's a very fine day!" said a timid voice at her side. She was walking by the White Rabbit, who was peeping anxiously into her face.

Alice thought she had never seen such a curious croquet-ground in her life; it was all ridges and furrows; the croquet balls were live hedgehogs, and the mallets live flamingoes, and the soldiers had to double themselves up and stand on their hands and feet, to make the arches. Alice soon came to the conclusion that it was a very difficult game indeed. The players all played at once, without waiting for turns, quarreling all the while, and fighting for the hedgehogs; and in a very short time the Queen was in a furious passion. "They're dreadfully fond of beheading people here; the great wonder is, that there's any one left alive!"

120

121

She was looking about for some way of escape, and wondering whether she could get away without being seen, when she noticed a curious appearance in the air; it puzzled her very much at first, but after watching it a minute or two she made it out to be a grin, and she said to herself, "It's the Cheshire Cat; now I shall have somebody to talk to."

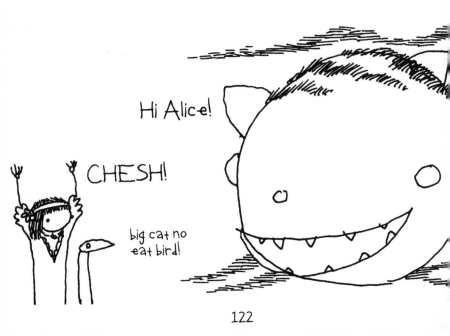

Hi Alice!

CHESH!

big cat no eat bird!

123

"Who are you talking to?" said the King, coming up to Alice, and looking at the Cat's head with great curiosity.

"It's a friend of mine—a Cheshire Cat," said Alice.

"I don't like the look of it at all," said the King, "and don't look at me like that!" He got behind Alice as he spoke.

"A cat may look at a king," said Alice.

"Well it must be removed," said the King, and he called to the Queen who was passing at the moment, "My dear! I wish you would have this cat removed!"

The Queen had only one way of settling all difficulties, great or small. "Off with his head!" she said, without even looking round.

"I'll fetch the executioner myself," said the King eagerly, and he hurried off.

Kiss my ring.

I'd rather not

oh gosh . . .

The game was in such confusion that she never knew whether it was her turn or not. So she went off in search of her hedgehog.

When she got back to the Cheshire Cat, she was surprised to find quite a large crowd collected round it; there was a dispute going on between the executioner, the King, and the Queen, who were all talking at once, while all the rest were quite silent, and looked very uncomfortable. The moment Alice appeared, she was appealed to by all three to settle the question. The executioner's argument was, that you couldn't cut off a head unless there was a body to cut it off from. The King's argument was, that anything that had a head could be beheaded. The Queen's argument was, that if something wasn't done about it in less than no time, she'd have everybody executed, all round.

126

THE CAT BELONGS TO THE DUCHESS!
BETTER ASK HER!

Go get the Duchess then!
Is she still with her head?

And the executioner went
off like an arrow. The Cat's head
began fading away the moment
he was gone, and, by the time he
had come back with the Duchess,
it had entirely disappeared; so
the King and the executioner
ran wildly up and down, looking
for it, while the rest of the party
went back to the game.

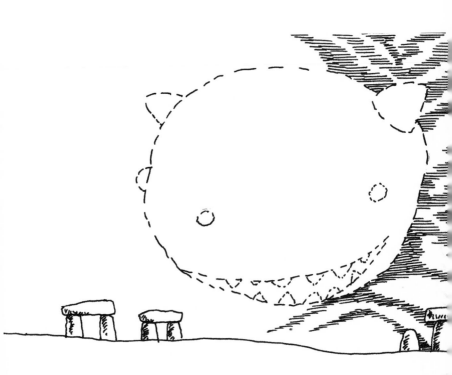

CHAPTER NINE:
the mock turtle's story

"You can't think how glad I am to see you again, you dear old thing!" said the Duchess, as she tucked her arm affectionately into Alice's, and they walked off together.

Alice was very glad to find her in such a pleasant temper, and thought to herself that perhaps it was only the pepper that had made her so savage when they met in the kitchen.

You're thinking about something my dear, and that makes you forget to talk. I can't tell you now what the moral of this is, but I shall remember in a bit.

Nice finger . . .

"Everything's got a moral, if only you can find it." And she squeezed herself up closer to Alice's side as she spoke. Alice did not much like her keeping so close to her; first, because the Duchess was very ugly; and secondly, because she was exactly the right height to rest her chin on Alice's shoulder, and it was an uncomfortably sharp chin. However, she did not like to be rude; so she bore it as well as she could.

Does your flamingo bite? Flamingoes and mustard both bite. And the moral of that is- Birds of a feather flock together.

Yeah . . . only mustard isn't a bird. Can you even hear yourself?

. . . seriously!

Alice looked up, and there stood the Queen in front of them, with her arms folded.

She's frowning like a thunderstorm . . .

Now I give you fair warning, either you or your head must be off, and that in about half of no time! Take your choice!

The Duchess took her choice, and was gone in a moment.

"Let's go on with the game," the Queen said to Alice; and Alice was too much frightened to say a word, but slowly followed her back to the croquet-ground. The other guests had taken advantage of the Queen's absence, and were resting in the shade. However, the moment they saw her, they hurried back to the game, the Queen merely remarking that a moment's delay would cost them their lives.

All the time they were playing, the Queen never left off quarreling with the other players, and shouting "Off with his head!" or "Off with her head!" Those whom she sentenced were taken into custody by the soldiers, who of course had to leave off being arches to do this, so that, by the end of half an hour or so, there were no arches left, and all the players, except the King, the Queen, and Alice, were in custody and under sentence of execution.

OFF WITH THEIR HEADS!
OFF WITH THEIR HEADS!
Hey, have you seen the Mock
Turtle yet? They're what
Mock Turtle soup is made from.

As they walked off together, Alice heard the King say in a low voice, to the company generally, "You are all pardoned."

They very soon came upon a Gryphon, lying fast asleep in the sun. (If you don't know what a Gryphon is, look at the picture.)

Wake up lazy thing! Take this girl to see the Mock Turtle and to hear its history. I must go back and see after some executions.

Alice did not quite like the look of the creature, but on the whole she thought it would be quite as safe to stay with it as to go after that savage Queen; so she waited.

The Gryphon sat up and rubbed its eyes: then it watched the Queen till she was out of sight: then it chuckled. "What fun!" said the Gryphon, half to itself, half to Alice.

"What is the fun?" said Alice.

That Queen is all an act you know ... Nobody ever loses their head.

They had not gone far before they saw the Mock Turtle in the distance, sitting sad and lonely on a little ledge of rock, and, as they came nearer, Alice could hear him sighing as if his heart would break. She pitied him deeply. "What is his sorrow?"

"Once," said the Mock Turtle at last, with a deep sigh, "I was a real Turtle."

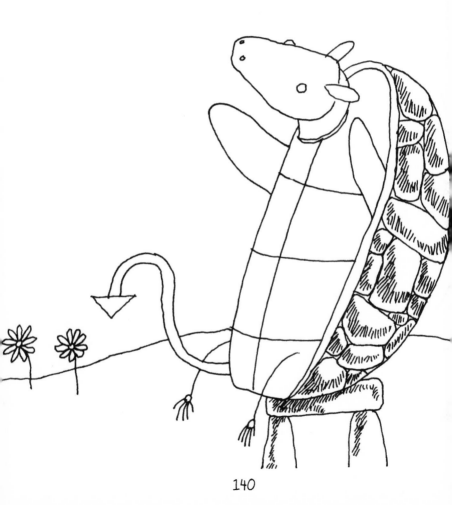

"When we were little, we went to school in the sea. I only took the regular course."

"What was that?" inquired Alice.

"Reeling and Writing, of course, to begin with," the Mock Turtle replied.

Then I learned about the different branches of arithmetic–Ambition, Distraction, Uglification, and Derision . . .

I have never heard of uglification.

dopey...

She is such a simpleton... HAHAHA!
That's enough about your lessons—tell
her about the games now.

142

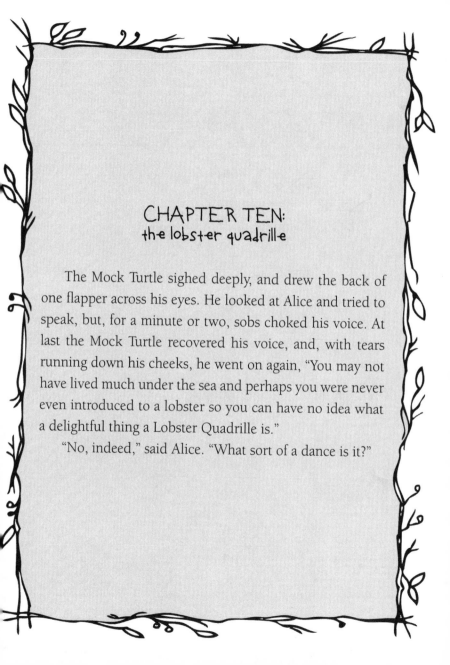

CHAPTER TEN:
the lobster quadrille

The Mock Turtle sighed deeply, and drew the back of one flapper across his eyes. He looked at Alice and tried to speak, but, for a minute or two, sobs choked his voice. At last the Mock Turtle recovered his voice, and, with tears running down his cheeks, he went on again, "You may not have lived much under the sea and perhaps you were never even introduced to a lobster so you can have no idea what a delightful thing a Lobster Quadrille is."

"No, indeed," said Alice. "What sort of a dance is it?"

You can show me the dance but if you call me stupid again, I will grow big and eat you in a soup!

I'll have some . . .

"You form two lines along the seashore . . . seals, turtles, salmon, and so on; then, when you've cleared all the jelly-fish out of the way . . . you advance twice, each with a lobster as a partner! Change lobsters, and retire in the same order, then you know, you throw the lobsters as far out to sea as you can . . . swim after them . . . turn a somersault in the sea, change lobsters again, back to land again, and—that's all the first figure."

147

Do you want us to show you a little bit—you don't even need a lobster.

That's insanity!

148

. . . The Mock Turtle sang this, very slowly and sadly;

'Will you walk a little faster?' said a whiting to a snail,
'There's a porpoise close behind us, and he's treading on my tail.
See how eagerly the lobsters and the turtles all advance!
They are waiting on the shingle—will you come and join the dance?
Will you, won't you, will you, won't you, will you join the dance?
Will you, won't you, will you, won't you, won't you join the dance?

'You really have no notion of how delightful it will be
When they take us up and throw us, with the lobsters, out to sea!'
But the snail replied, 'Too far, too far!' and gave a look askance—
Said he thanked the whiting kindly, but he would not join the dance.
Would not, could not, would not, could not, could not join the dance.
Would not, could not, would not, could not, could not join the dance.

'What matters is how far we go?' His scaly friend replied.
There is another shore, you know, upon the other side.
The further off from England the nearer is to France—
Then turn not pale, beloved snail, but come and join the dance.

Will you, won't you, will you, won't you, will you join the dance?
Will you, won't you, will you, won't you, won't you join the dance?'

I know I wouldn't . . .

149

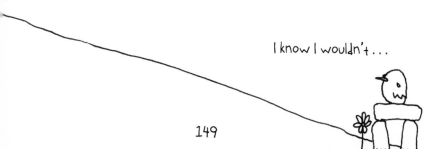

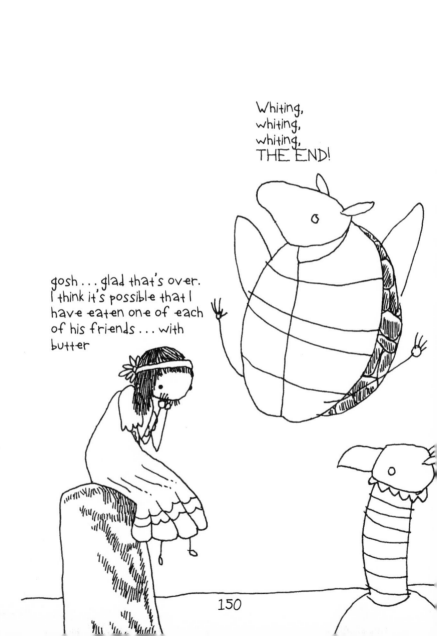

150

The Gryphon said, "Come, let's hear some of *your* adventures."

I could tell you my adventures—beginning from this morning, but it's no use going back to yesterday, because I was a different person then.

Explain all that!

Her listeners were perfectly quiet till she got to the part about her repeating "You are old, Father William" to the Caterpillar, and the words all coming different, and then the Mock Turtle drew a long breath, and said, "That's very curious!"

"It's all about as curious as it can be," said the Gryphon.

"It all came different!" the Mock Turtle repeated thoughtfully. "I should like to hear her try and repeat something now. Tell her to begin." He looked at the Gryphon as if he thought it had some kind of authority over Alice.

"Stand up and repeat "Tis the voice of the sluggard,'" said the Gryphon.

She got up, and began to repeat it, but her head was so full of the Lobster Quadrille, that she hardly knew what she was saying; and the words came very queer indeed:

'Tis the voice of the lobster;
I heard him declare
you have baked me too brown,
I must sugar my hair.
As a duck with his eyelids,
so he with his nose.
Trims his belt with his buttons,
and turns out his toes.

That's all wrong!

No good, no good!

153

"Shall we try another figure of the Lobster Quadrille?" the Gryphon went on. "Or would you like the Mock Turtle to sing you another song?"

"Oh, a song, please, if the Mock Turtle would be so kind," Alice replied.

Ahemmm... Turtle Soup. By Mock Turtle... here goes. Wait-can I stand up there? You got to stand up there...

Beautiful Soup, so rich and green,
Waiting in a hot tureen!
Who for such dainties would not stoop?
Soup of the evening, beautiful Soup!
Soup of the evening, beautiful Soup!

Beau-ootiful Soo-oop!
Beau-ootiful Soo-oop!
Soo-oop of the e-e-evening,
Beautiful, beautiful, Soup!

Beautiful Soup, who cares for fish,
Game, or any dish?
Who else would not give for two
Pennyworth only of beautiful Soup?
Pennyworth only of beautiful Soup?

Beau-ootiful Soo-oop!
Beau-ootiful Soo-oop!
Soo-oop of the e-e-evening,
Beautiful, beauti-FUL SOUP!

see . . . I want soup now.
That always happens.

155

The Mock Turtle had just begun to repeat it, when a cry of "The trial's beginning!" was heard in the distance.

"Come on!" cried the Gryphon, and, taking Alice by the hand, it hurried off.

The trial.

Thee trial.

whaaat trial?

CHAPTER ELEVEN:
who stole the tarts?

The King and Queen of Hearts were seated on their throne when they arrived, with a great crowd assembled about them—all sorts of little birds and beasts, as well as the whole pack of cards. The Knave was standing before them, in chains, with a soldier on each side to guard him; and near the King was the White Rabbit, with a trumpet in one hand, and a scroll of parchment in the other. Alice had never been in a court of justice before, but she had read about them in books, and she was quite pleased to find that she knew the name of nearly everything there. "That's the judge," she said to herself, "because of his great wig."

The judge, by the way, was the King; and, as he wore his crown over the wig. "And that's the jury-box," thought Alice; "and those twelve creatures, I suppose they are the jurors." She said this last word two or three times over to herself, being rather proud of it; for she thought, and rightly too, that very few little girls of her age knew the meaning of it at all.

I hope this is a speedy trial and they hand out refreshments soon.

The twelve jurors were all writing very busily on slates.

"Herald, read the accusation!" said the King. On this the White Rabbit blew three blasts on the trumpet, and then unrolled the parchment-scroll, and read:

The Queen of Hearts,
she made some tarts
All on a summer day;
The Knave of Hearts
he stole the tarts,
and took them quite away!

FIRRRRST WITNESS!!!

The first witness was the Hatter.

Take off your hat and give your evidence or I'll execute you on the spot!

I beg pardon, your Majesty, for bringing these in; but I hadn't quite finished my tea when I was sent for.

Watch your neck Hatter . . .

Just at this moment Alice felt a very curious sensation, which puzzled her a good deal until she made out what it was; she was beginning to grow larger again, and she thought at first she would get up and leave the court; but on second thoughts she decided to remain where she was as long as there was room for her.

Alice goes up . . . again.

What's wrong with that girl?

Always making a scene, Alice.

"You've no right to grow *here*," said the Dormouse.

"Don't talk nonsense," said Alice more boldly; "you know *you're* growing too."

"Yes, but I grow at a reasonable pace," said the Dormouse; "not in that ridiculous fashion." And he got up very sulkily and crossed over to the other side of the court.

165

Oh gosh, you are a poor man and a poor speaker... thanks for nothing, Hatter! Call the next witness!

NEXT WITNESS!!!

Oh thank goodness. Another day of having a head to drink my tea with. Hey, where's the Dormouse going?

The next witness was the Duchess's cook. She carried the pepper-box in her hand, and Alice guessed who it was, even before she got into the court, by the way the people near the door began sneezing all at once.

Cook-what are the
tarts made of?

achooooo!

pepper mostly...

167

For some minutes the whole court was in confusion, getting the Dormouse turned out, and, by the time they had settled down again, the cook had disappeared.

"Never mind!" said the King, with an air of great relief. "Call the next witness."

Call it loud Rabbit-So
the people in the back
can hear you!

Allllllliiiiiic-e!

he called
Alice . . .
the girl!

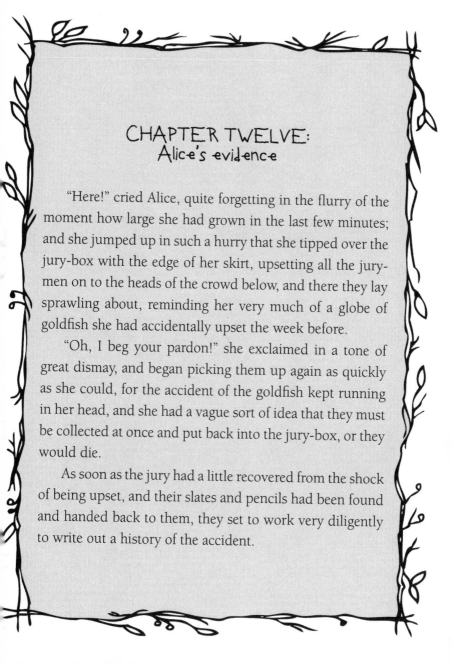

CHAPTER TWELVE:
Alice's evidence

"Here!" cried Alice, quite forgetting in the flurry of the moment how large she had grown in the last few minutes; and she jumped up in such a hurry that she tipped over the jury-box with the edge of her skirt, upsetting all the jury-men on to the heads of the crowd below, and there they lay sprawling about, reminding her very much of a globe of goldfish she had accidentally upset the week before.

"Oh, I beg your pardon!" she exclaimed in a tone of great dismay, and began picking them up again as quickly as she could, for the accident of the goldfish kept running in her head, and she had a vague sort of idea that they must be collected at once and put back into the jury-box, or they would die.

As soon as the jury had a little recovered from the shock of being upset, and their slates and pencils had been found and handed back to them, they set to work very diligently to write out a history of the accident.

There you go, back in place. What a strange little bugger you are.

What do you know of this business?

Nothing whatever!

SILENCE! Rule Forty-Two. All persons more than a mile high must leave the court!

I am not a mile high . . .

You are!

Nearly two miles!

175

Well I thought it was a letter written by the Knave-but it's actually a set of verses.

off wi...

This makes you more guilty!

Please your Majesty, I didn't write it and they can't prove I did. There's no name signed at the end.

176

"Read them," said the King.

The White Rabbit put on his spectacles. "Where shall I begin, please your Majesty?" he asked.

"Begin at the beginning," the King said, very gravely, "and go on till you come to the end; then stop." There was dead silence in the court, whilst the White Rabbit read out these verses:

"They told me you had been to her,
And mentioned me to him;
She gave me a good character,
But said I could not swim.

He sent them word I had not gone
(we know it to be true)
If she would push the matter on,
What would become of you?

I gave her one, they gave him two,
You gave us three or more;
They all returned from him to you,
Though they were mine before.

If I or she should chance to be
involved in this affair,
He trusts to you to set them free,
Exactly as we were.

My notion was that you had been
(Before she had this fit)
An obstacle that came between
Him, and ourselves, and it.

Don't let him know she liked them best,
For this must ever be
A secret, kept from all the rest,
Between yourself and me."

177

Alice had grown so large in the last few minutes that she wasn't a bit afraid of interrupting.

If anyone can explain it, I'll give him sixpence. I don't believe there's an ATOM of meaning in it!

That's the most important piece of evidence yet! Now let the jury . . .

You guys find any atoms?

I s-e-em to see some meaning in them after all. "Said I could not swim"—you can't swim, can you?

STUFF AND NONSENSE!

The idea of giving a sentence first! This whole trial is insane . . . I should take your little head off . . . ohhhh I'm so angry right now I could just . . .

HOLD YOUR TONGUE!!!
OFF WITH HER HEAD!!
OFF WITH HER HEAD!!!

"Who cares for you?" said Alice. "You're nothing but a pack of cards!" At this the whole pack rose up into the air, and came flying down upon her; she gave a little scream, half of fright and half of anger, and tried to beat them off.

nooooooooooooo!

She found herself lying on the bank, with her head in the lap of her sister, who was gently brushing away some dead leaves that had fluttered down from the trees upon her face.

Wake up Alice my dear.
Why, what a long sleep you've had.

huh?

alic

alic-e!

alic-e!

"Oh, I've had such a curious dream!" said Alice; and she told her sister, as well as she could remember them, all these strange adventures of hers that you have just been reading about; and, when she had finished, her sister kissed her, and said,

Mother has fixed the afternoon tea.
Now go inside and relax. Mr. Dodgson will
be stopping over to take your portrait.

Oh ok . . . I suppose tea would
help. I wonder if Mr. Dodgson
will want to hear my story?

So Alice got up and ran off, thinking while she ran, as well she might, what a wonderful dream it had been.

Puck —
Your cat should
be able to find almost
everything it ever
wanted to know in
here —
love
Bets
11/8/76

Faith McNulty and
Elisabeth Keiffer

Wholly Cats

Drawings by Peggy Bacon

GRAMERCY PUBLISHING COMPANY

NEW YORK

To Morris and Lottie Povar

Authors' Note

This book is a collaboration. As we are sisters, we have had the opportunity to share the acquaintance of a good many cats. In writing *Wholly Cats*, however, the work seemed to divide naturally into two parts. Part I, the practical and the particular, was written by Elisabeth Keiffer. Part II, a more general view of the feline family, was written by Faith Mc-Nulty.

Familiarity with cats, no matter how affectionate one feels toward them, cannot take the place of scientific research. The medical sections of this book are the result of still another collaboration—with Dr. Morris Povar, associate in research in the Institute of Health Sciences at Brown University. With his brother, Dr. Povar runs the Povar Animal Hospital in East Providence, Rhode Island. He not only was generous enough to share his medical knowledge and his experience as a practicing veterinarian with the authors, but gave much of his time to the difficult process of putting technical information into terms useful to the layman.

Library of Congress Catalog Card Number: 62–10018

Copyright © MCMLXII by Faith McNulty

Printed in the United States of America

This edition published by Gramercy Publishing Co.,
a division of Crown Publishers, Inc., by
arrangement with Bobbs-Merrill Co., Inc.
(A)

Contents

CATS IN GENERAL

Chapter I

Upon Meeting a Cat

Almost everyone knows something about cats, simply because there are so many of them. There are millions in the United States alone; perhaps not quite as many as people, but certainly more than enough to go around. Cats are part of every civilized society and have been for thousands of years.

Since a passing familiarity with cats is easily come by, there is a widespread notion that there is little more to them than meets the eye. I shared this idea for a good many years and thought, too, that my lifelong friendship with cats had made me more than ordinarily knowledgeable. Not until I began to look into the formal literature on cats did I realize

15

how large and how technical the subject is. A glance at the research that has been done on the feline family humbled me rapidly.

Despite the amount of study devoted to cats, the subject still abounds in mystery and controversy. Where, for instance, did the present-day domestic cat come from? Out of the deserts of Egypt, with the blood of European wild cats added later, or were cats domesticated independently in different parts of the world? It is a puzzle on which eminent authorities still differ. Then, on the purely practical level, such a seemingly innocent question as the effect of mashed potatoes on kitty's digestion can be debated as hotly as permissive child rearing.

To begin by taking nothing for granted seemed to me the most logical way to get a grip on the cat. This book is, then, for people like myself, admirers of the cat (I hesitate to call them cat-lovers since a grammatical purist has pointed out that a horse-lover is a horse in love with another horse) in whom affectionate but unscientific acquaintanceship has stirred a desire to know more, both practical and impractical.

If this assumption of ignorance insults some knowledgeable readers, perhaps they can nevertheless be provided a few tidbits they mightn't have run across. Does everyone know that the position of the third eyelid of a cat, the nictitating membrane or haw, as it is sometimes called, can be an indication that the cat harbors worms?

Then there is the theory that the first cat came not from Egypt, but was created in response to the first human need for a mouse trap. It seems that during Noah's voyage the mouse problem got out of hand. Noah begged the lioness for help. She obligingly sneezed and brought forth the first cat. After learning this I have noticed that my cat gives expectant and wondering attention to anyone who sneezes in her presence.

16

The hairs inside a cat's ear are designed to discourage exploration by insects, but the purpose of the little pocket or double fold at the edge of the ear has not been mentioned by the authorities I have consulted. This forces me to rely on the explanation given me years ago by a know-it-all playmate who insisted the pocket was to hold the cat's spare thoughts, thriftily saved for rainy-day meditation.

We all know that a cat's eyes shine in the dark, but does everyone know that the glow is caused by the reflection of light from a membrane behind the retina called the *tapetum lucidum?* The color of the glow is usually greenish or golden, but the eyes of the Siamese reflect a luminous ruby red. I was happy, too, to add to my vocabulary the handsome word chatoyant which means to shine like a cat's eyes in the dark.

But, since practical things should come first, let us assume that the reader, a kind-hearted potential friend of cats, who has inexplicably been isolated from contact with them, is suddenly the surprised and anxious custodian of one. The first and vital question is what to do upon becoming the owner of a cat for the first time?

The first problem that would worry a person in such a fix is how to get the cat to stop walking around, lashing its tail and wailing. The behavior of a cat on arriving in a strange home is in every way calculated to make a new owner nervous. It is perhaps the only occasion on which a cat can be said to be truly tactless. It stalks about inspecting everything and uttering what might be taken as bitter complaints and unflattering comments on the deplorable conditions it finds at every hand.

If you have put out a welcoming lunch, the cat may sniff it, register disgust, and stalk on. This doesn't mean that the cat is sick or that your cooking is terrible, but merely that the cat is too jittery to eat or has just been fed. The cat will

17

quite likely go under your bed and come out again with an expression that might make you hesitate to look under it yourself. From there, it may bound to the mantelpiece but, finding your ornaments disappointing, thump to the floor, only to leap to the window sill and stare out longingly at the world of the unconfined. Perhaps it will shrug off your welcoming caresses, leaving you with fingers full of hair and a growing doubt that the two of you are ever going to get together.

But all this will pass; perhaps in an hour or two, certainly in a day or two.

I am not among those cat authorities whose gifts include reading the minds of cats, but it is not unreasonable or anthropomorphic to guess that the cat is wondering where in God's name it is and what is going to happen next. With this on its mind, it has no time for courtesies. In cold, clear words taken from a veterinary manual, "house cats are a domesticated variety of a wild species which exhibits an inconsistent acceptance of human beings."

In other words, cats lose their heads under stress. Their trust in people is no more than skin-deep, and a frightened cat can forget in an instant everything it ever knew about civilized relationships. In a tight spot a cat relies only on itself and its instinctive defenses: to run, to hide, to climb and to fight when cornered. Then, because cats are inconsistent, it can become appreciative, friendly and trustful as soon as the crisis is over. The fact that a newly-arrived cat behaves like a little jaguar just trapped in the jungle is not necessarily an indication that it will never be tame. It is more a measure of how frightening the cat has found the journey to your home.

Cats prefer traveling under their own steam and approach the idea of riding in trains, planes, automobiles or on horseback with suspicion. (If our superstitious forefathers had thought it over they would have realized that no cat could have been persuaded to ride on a witch's broomstick). But cats are learning animals. If their first experience of involuntary travel is particularly alarming, they will dread it ever after. On the other hand, if the first trip turns out pleasantly, they will come to tolerate travel, or even to enjoy it.

Although cats do like small spaces, caves of their own choosing, they know a trap when they see one. They like boxes, but they hate being locked into one. A cat that has been popped into a small box for the first time, fastened in, and joggled about during the trip to your home is likely to shoot out like a rocket the moment the lid is lifted. Its instinct then is to keep going while the going is good. It is in no mood for caresses or soft words. For this reason it is well to give some thought to where you first let the cat out.

Don't, of course, open the cat-box outdoors. You may never see more of the cat than a streak of flying fur, or you may spend hours or days trying to get it down from a treetop or out from under the woodpile. I once lost a beautiful cat just this way—a handsome young Abyssinian that had been shipped in a crate from the West Coast to New York. The airplane trip had frightened her terribly. During the taxi ride from the airport to my apartment, I foolishly opened the box to try to comfort her. When we alighted, she instantly squirmed out of my grasp and was gone like an arrow down Third Avenue. I soon lost the trail in a maze of backyards and, to my sorrow, never saw her again.

The best place to let a cat out of its box is in a small room (a room without a fireplace into which the cat can wedge itself), where you can leave it shut up for a while to settle down. In my house, this would be the bathroom, or, better yet, the screened porch. A newly-arrived cat seems to feel that its first job is to investigate every aspect of its new surroundings, and it won't have much time for you until the job is completed. If it is kept in one room, the cat's task is simplified. It can look over the rest of the house later when it has achieved a more tranquil state of mind. If the cat does have the run of the house, be sure all the windows are shut.

Let us hope that very shortly the new cat will let you pet it a bit, but don't be too hurt if it won't. (If, after two weeks, however, the cat still rejects all your overtures, you have picked a lemon in the garden of cats. What you do about it is a moral question beyond the scope of my advice, but in truth I've never heard of such a case.)

If there is a dog in residence at the time of the cat's arrival, do not have the dog participate in welcoming the cat. There could be no worse way to initiate a relationship than by allowing a surprised dog to meet a scared cat. Shut the dog up, out of earshot, if possible, or send it over to the neighbor's house to play, and don't let them meet until the cat feels it has charge of itself and its surroundings.

This advice about dogs also applies, unfortunately, to any small child you may have around the house. Even if the child is to be titular owner of the cat, it is best not to let him take possession until you have paved the way. I do not believe that children have a natural instinct for handling animals. In fact, I believe quite the opposite. It usually takes considerable counseling, cautioning and example-setting to get a child to handle animal in an acceptable way; acceptable to the cat, that is. When a new cat arrives, the child will be just as excited as the cat and expect it to adore him instantly. If the child is allowed to open the box, the cat will pop out. There will be a flurry as the child dives for the cat. The cat will scratch the child, and outrage will be mutual. Should the new arrival be a small kitten, a child is apt to squeeze it too hard, or drop it in fright when it scratches. All in all, the meeting of cat and child requires almost as much tact as the introduction of cat and dog.

The room in which you first keep the cat must have some sanitary facilities. If the cat has been previously housebroken, it would be well to find out to what sort of material, or litter, as it is unfortunately called in the trade, the cat has been accustomed. If you can't find out or haven't got the stuff, then torn-up newspapers in a cardboard box are the handiest expedient. In the country, soft earth, gravel or sand may be at hand. If you do not provide something, the cat is likely to choose the fireplace, someone's bed, or the bathtub. The latter, horrid as it may sound, is to my mind less disastrous than some other spots it might pick, since with hot water and cleansing powder the deed can be undone without leaving a trace. Even if you intend that ultimately the cat's toilet will be out-of-doors, do not let the cat out for this purpose until you are sure that you will be able to get it back without a struggle.

When you shut the cat up, don't forget to leave it a dish of water. Perhaps the fact that cats don't like to bathe has given rise to the popular assumption that they don't drink water either. It isn't so; milk is not a substitute. The cat should be offered both, but water is the more important.

So, having left the cat alone with its thoughts and a dish of water, look in the refrigerator to see what there is that might cheer the newcomer.

Whatever you serve, don't serve it ice cold. If the cat has been starved, don't give it too much. The cat may overeat and throw up. The whole subject of cat diet is one which authorities treat with considerable gravity, and there have been as many fads and controversies in cat feeding as in human nutrition. Its complexities will be taken up later on, since we are speaking here only of the first meal rustled up in an emergency. From the cat's point of view, the nicest thing would be a small sirloin steak served raw; however, it will gratefully accept any kind of meat, raw or cooked. A cat enjoys chunks, but in the course of enjoyment may drag them all over the floor, leaving greasy trails, so people usually unfeelingly cut the meat up. If you serve chicken or fresh fish, remove the bones. Canned tuna fish is all right; sardines are pretty rich fare. Canned dog food also will do. Should there be a baby in the house, a can of baby meat (I don't mean meat *of* baby but *for* baby—I'm not that far gone about cats) would be fine. So, of course, would any prepared cat food. Failing all these possibilities, a soft-boiled egg is the next choice. It may be mixed with a little cooked cereal to stretch it a bit. Cereal foods are at the bottom of the cat's list of preferences and are often refused unless mixed with something tastier. Cereal foods include rice, mashed potatoes, bread and other starches. A predominantly starchy meal will give the cat a poor impression of your cuisine.

A cat's bed is usually the least of its worries, so it is not necessary to provide it with an innerspring mattress for its first night's sleep under your roof. It will sleep on the floor, a chair, or on top of the laundry hamper, but it should be able to get out of a draft and it will appreciate an old pillow, or a blanket or even a bath towel, particularly if the weather is cold.

The polite way to go about picking up a shy cat is to extend a hand and hope that after the cat has smelled your fingers it will let you stroke it for a minute; then slip a hand under its belly so that you clasp the cat to you with your fingers supporting its chest. If a cat is too wild or frightened to allow this, it may be necessary to take the classic grip on the scruff of the neck. It won't injure the cat, but it certainly won't endear you to it, and you will find that you can't carry a heavy cat in this fashion for more than a few steps before it squirms out of your grasp. If you must carry a wild or recalcitrant cat for any distance, it would be better to put it in a box or sack. If you have nothing else suitable, you might consider a pillow case or a shirt with the neck buttoned and the sleeves tied together.

If your new boarder is not a cat but a kitten, it is in many ways much easier to get through the stage of first acquaintance—in fact, there may be nothing to it. A kitten, however, will need more time and care, and not every kitten is immediately loving and cuddly. A kitten that has been raised by a wild mother with the woodpile for a nursery will spit and fight with admirable though largely impotent fury. It will also get over its suspicions more quickly than an older cat. Food is the way to its heart. If a kitten is less than eight weeks old, it should not have left its mother. If, nonetheless, it has left its mother and it is up to you to raise it, turn to Chapter IV, "Love and Consequences," on the care of infants. An older kitten can be fed more or less like an adult except that its food should be finer and mushier—moistened with broth or milk—and its meals more frequent.

A kitten needs warmth, and the thing it misses most is being one of a bundle of furry bodies. A hot water bottle in its bed will console it if it seems very shivery and miserable and so, too, will lots of lap-sitting. If this is the kitten's first experience away from its family, it may be very lonely and look to you to fill the void. A small kitten that haunts your footsteps is easy to step on. I have stepped on more than one small, clinging kitten, though only lightly, I'm happy to say.

Warmth and a full belly are what put a kitten to sleep; therefore it might be a good idea to time things so that the last meal coincides with your bedtime and you can retire without the mewing of a melancholy baby ringing in your ears. If the kitten is so lonesome it wakes you up in the middle of the night and won't go back to sleep, wrap an alarm clock in a towel and put it in the kitten's bed. The tick-tick works like phenobarbital.

Finally, it may be that fate has singled you out (as it has me, numerous times) to provide a home for a poor, hungry stray whose sorry condition wrings your heart at the same time as it makes you somewhat nervous about clasping to your bosom so many fleas, and possibly germs. Your first impulse then may be to pop the cat and its fleas into the tub for a good wash. (If there is a child at hand, the child will urge you on. Children love prescribing baths. I recently found my son washing his unfortunate white rat.) But it is best to hold off unless the cat is extremely dirty and extremely docile. Bathing a cat is quite a project. Given a few days in a clean environment, a dirty cat can clean itself up remarkably. If the cat will let you brush and flea-powder it (see Chapter V), that will be a big help and you can save the bath until your relationship can better stand the strain. Fleas are supposed to be undiscriminating in their tastes, but in my impetuous, unfastidious youth I embraced many a sleazy, fleasy kitten and as far as I was aware the fleas always preferred the cat.

It is, of course, nice to get rid of the fleas, but it needn't be done in the first five minutes. As for diseases, there are not many that a human is likely to catch from a cat. Ringworm may be transmitted from human to cat and vice versa and is the only one common enough to worry about. Mange is quite rare. Sore places and a mangy look are more likely to be due to cuts and insect bites. If you suspect your stray may have ailments other than malnutrition, you should take it to a veterinarian for a thorough going-over and worming if that seems necessary.

These introductory words may be elementary to many and may also have painted rather a dark picture of the first few days of cat ownership. In trying to cover the more trying contingencies, the reader may have gained the impression that the burdens are many and the joys few. In fact, the reverse is true, but the pleasures of having a cat seem so obvious and so personal that I don't feel I should intrude into this intimate realm. Suffice it to say that though the rewards of liking cats elude some people entirely, to many it is one of life's gentlest and most easily accessible joys. It costs little, can last a lifetime, and the doctor won't order you to give it up. Fortunately, analysis really isn't needed. I'm not sure myself why I so deeply enjoy having cats—along with many other kinds of pets. Not knowing why detracts nothing. I'm merely grateful that I do.

Chapter II

Home Is Where the Cat Is

Life with a cat can have a number of different aspects; the pleasures and problems vary, depending on whether the surroundings are a city apartment, a country cottage or a traveling box. But the basic requirement to domestic tranquillity in any environment is some understanding of the cat's mind. Once that is achieved, mutually satisfactory standards of behavior can be established.

The cat's mind is by no means easy to read; it does not

26

work like the dog's mind. Dogs are used to living in packs, and subservience to a pack leader or human master is native to them. Cats have survived through the ages as solitary hunters, dependent on no one. Blind obedience is not their forte.

Nor does the feline mind resemble the human, and it is a waste of time to try to judge it by human standards. In the nineteenth century, the popular view of animals was anthropomorphic, ascribing to them such purely human traits as selfishness, heartlessness, indifference, and so on. Then a reaction set in; scientists began trying to evaluate animal behavior and measure animal intelligence entirely in terms of such mechanical behavioral concepts as the conditioned reflex. With cats, this has been largely unsuccessful. Differences in motivation and emotional makeup make it practically impossible to devise standardized tests that compare felines meaningfully with other animals. Somewhere between these extremes lies the path to understanding feline behavior, but like everything else these days it is a far more complex subject than was once realized.

Some facts, however, have been successfully established by laboratory research. One, equally well known to any person who has had an acquaintanceship with cats, is that they vary enormously as individuals. Not only do they vary in likes and dislikes, habits, vocabularies and tolerances, but seem to vary in their motivations, as well. We also know, without scientists telling us, that cats can learn. How much they learn depends on the cat. A marked trait of the feline, though, is what scientists call perseveration and what we might call a determination to stick-to-it-right-or-wrong. Repeated experiments have shown that if a cat prefers a triangle instead of a circle on the first try, in subsequent choices it will stick to the triangle long after a dog or a monkey has changed its preference to win the reward. Quite possibly there is some connection between this and the fact that a cat that has messed in some forbidden spot once is very likely to keep repeating its mistake, no matter how indignant its master nor how severely it is punished. Knowing this, people experienced with cats, instead of simply punishing them, take great pains to make sure the cat has no opportunity to repeat the mistake until the impulse is forgotten. They may barricade the spot, scrub and douse it with cat-repellent or place the cat's pan over it, if that is feasible.

In experimental psychology, reasoning in animals is considered to be insight as to cause and effect. In practical terms, this means the extent to which the animal understands the relationship between crime and punishment. I do not know how the cat scores in laboratory tests; my own opinion is that it connects crime with punishment less easily than the dog, not necessarily because of lower intelligence but because of different motivation. What this means to the owner of a cat is that training is not always simple. Punishment works with some cats, but then only if it is instant, severe, and invariable, and these are qualifications one usually can't or doesn't want to fulfill. If, for example, every time the cat pounced on a bird it got a severe electrical shock, undoubtedly it would stop chasing birds. On the other hand, beating the cat when it comes home with a dead bird in its mouth is not going to convey the idea that birds are taboo, but simply that people are mean.

An old hand with cats once explained to me that they always do what they want to do. The secret of training them, she said, was to make them want to do what you wanted them to do—a clear example of one-upmanship, and perhaps an oversimplification, but certainly a more practical approach than stubbornly pitting your will against the cat's, a contest the cat usually wins.

One reason that people value cats so highly as pets is that they fit so comfortably into human households. There are really very few points on which discipline has to be established. The most vital is housebreaking. Others that come quickly to mind are: training a cat not to claw furniture to shreds, not to jump on the dining table, to eat what it is given, and to play gently. The cat's reaction is different to each of these matters, so a training approach must vary somewhat in each instance.

Cats instinctively want to be clean, not only in their persons but in their surroundings, and given any human cooperation at all, they almost always will be. This is why the right toilet arrangements are so necessary, not only to the cat's owner, but to the cat. The cat's requisites are not hard to fill; because felines instinctively bury their excretions, the cat wants something it can scratch in, it would like room to turn around in and some privacy, and it wants a pan that is always in the same place and does not have a bad smell. On pans, there are two schools of thought. One holds out for metal trays like roasting pans; the other swears by cardboard cartons because they can be thrown out when they are dirty instead of having to be washed. In fact, a friend of mine spends a great deal of time scavenging Campbell Soup cartons, her favorites, for just this purpose. If you use a carton, put lots of newspaper or a sheet of foil underneath it; in either case, the container should be lined with newspaper to make emptying easier, with the scratchable stuff on top. Shredded paper, sand or sawdust will do in a pinch, but there is no denying that a much stronger smell emanates from both newspaper and sand than from a patented litter. A metal tray should be thoroughly scrubbed with hot water and soap about once a week. Disinfectants should not be used; their smell is unpleasant to cats and some are toxic.

If you fulfill these requirements, ordinarily there is little more to do except show the cat where the pan is. Most kittens are trained by their mothers, so by the time they go to a new home they know what a pan is for. However, not all mothers are equally efficient at this; sometimes you have to take up where they left off. And, occasionally, you run across a cat that just seems to be untrainable. Anyone living in an apartment may have no choice but to get rid of the cat; in the country it may be persuaded to use the great outdoors.

When it comes to clawing, you and the cat are on opposite sides of the fence. Cats need to claw; in the country they will, by preference, take this exercise on tree trunks. In the city their choice is limited. If nothing is provided, they will find something themselves to scratch on, and once they have established a preference, they don't give it up easily. Here, as in other aspects of training, it's important to get them on the right track at an early age. Most pet shops sell scratching posts; if you buy one make sure it is high enough so the cat can stand on its hind legs and stretch to full length to scratch and that it is sturdily made so it won't topple over on the cat. If that happens, the cat probably will never go near it again. Many people make their own scratching posts by mounting a log on a strong platform or by nailing uprights to a platform and covering them with carpeting. In that case, as my veterinarian sadly points out, they almost always put the carpeting on wrong. The under side, not the pile, should be exposed so the cat can dig its claws into the canvas. Catnip inside a scratching post makes it more alluring to many cats. The cat should be shown what the scratching post is for and consistently reprimanded if it uses anything else for the purpose. A sharp "No!" or a loud hand clap will usually put the idea across. Claw clipping and de-clawing are more extreme measures that can be taken if all else fails. (See Chapter V.)

Jumping on the dining room table or stealing food is such a natural feline instinct that it may take time and patience to train a cat that it mustn't do it. The moral implication of mine and thine is, after all, not something the feline mind can be expected to encompass. My method, which I admit calls for a good deal of vigilance, is to remove the cat promptly every time it jumps up, give it a light smack on the nose, and say "No" in a firm tone, coupled with its name. Cats seem to learn their names quite quickly and to understand an order more clearly when it is used. Some cats show considerable response to disapproval or a reproachful tone of voice; others are left utterly unmoved. The impervious feline is a difficult customer to train in this instance. I don't believe it is humane to spank a cat; and, in any case, it usually doesn't do any good. I have used successfully another method of dissuasion, which perhaps is just as mean; that is to keep a loaded water pistol handy and squirt the recalcitrant pussy whenever I catch it on the table.

When a cat plays so rough that it leaves its human playmate scratched and bleeding, it may be because it was taken from the litter before it learned good play manners with its siblings or because it was taught to as a kitten, by its owner. As a small girl I made this grievous mistake with my first puppy. It is one that is practically irreversible. When puppies and kittens are very young their teeth and claws don't inflict any pain to speak of and it is easy for both owner and animal to get carried away in wild games of pounce. Later these games cease to be any fun for the person, but by then the pet considers them *de rigueur* and is bewildered by a refusal to play. So, obviously, it is only fair and practical to teach kittens to play gently when they're little.

A household which includes a cat may also include another cat, a dog or children. Usually everyone lives together in blissful harmony. However, the proper introductions have a good deal to do with making this so. Some owners go to rather elaborate lengths when they acquire a new cat or kitten while another is in residence. Sometimes the two are kept shut up in separate rooms for several days on the theory that each will become so intrigued by the smell of the mysterious stranger next door that when they meet they will swoon into each other's arms. A simpler way is to produce the new incumbent at a propitious moment—not feeding time—keep a sharp eye on the strangers until you have an idea of how each reacts to the other, and be scrupulous in dividing your attention evenly between the two. It would be a serious mistake to feed the cats together; I usually put their dishes in separate rooms for a while. Once they have grown accustomed to each other they can be fed in the same room, but still in separate plates. How the cats will take to each other is almost impossible to predict. I am assuming, of course, that both cats, if they are full grown, are neutered. Sometimes a pair of cats become as devoted and dependent as an old married couple. Sometimes they never go beyond the point of barely tolerating each other. But they rarely fight so furiously or so continuously that it is impossible to keep both in the same household.

Although cats and dogs are natural enemies in the wild, in domestic life they are often inseparable friends or, at the least, share a home with cool politeness. My veterinarian owns a German shepherd that delights in grooming his two cats. Papoose adores these ministrations and sometimes returns them. It has taken Pancho a year to learn to suffer them without scratching, but Pancho is extremely eclectic in his tastes. Naturally, the temperament of both animals is the basic factor; a confirmed cat-chaser isn't going to make a pleasant companion for even the most tolerant cat. But again, a tactful introduction is most important in getting the relationship off to a good start.

Cats have to be protected from children far more often than children have to be protected from cats. I have never seen a cat in good health unprovokedly attack a child, whereas tail pulling, poking a finger in the eye, and squeezing indubitably amounts to attack, no matter how well intentioned. If cats really find children frightening, they usually take pains to keep out of their way. More often they will submit resignedly to indignities from a child that they wouldn't take from anyone grown. In this case, it's really the child who has to be trained, which is much harder than training a cat, God knows!

Cats do not suck the breath out of babies! In his book, *The Natural History of Nonsense*, Professor Bergen Evans cites this delusion as one of the most ancient and unfounded superstitions about felines, a survival, he surmises, of the old belief in vampires and succubi. Possibly a tiny infant might be smothered by a cat that got into its crib seeking warmth. This would be a hard charge to prove against the cat. Nevertheless, ordinary common sense should dictate that it is wiser not to have an infant and a cat share a bedroom.

Although a city apartment is as opposite to a cat's natural habitat as anything imaginable, the feline population in metropolitan centers is increasing every year. Because cats are small, clean, adaptable, and companionable, they make ideal city pets. However, if they are to stay healthy and everyone is to be happy, some modifications in their routine are necessary. Since an apartment-pent cat simply hasn't the opportunity to burn as many calories as an outdoor cat has, it should be fed more lightly. Nutrition and the dangers of obesity are taken up in the next chapter, as well as in Chapter VII. The city cat also lacks the opportunities for self-grooming that are afforded a country cat and needs more faithful brushing to prevent hairballs (see Chapter V) and spare the furniture. Proper toilet facilities for an indoor cat have already been mentioned, but in an apartment frequent changing of the pan is more necessary than ever. Like the girl in the mouthwash ad, a cat owner is often the last to realize that the apartment smells to high heaven; sometimes the truth doesn't dawn until all non-cat friends have stopped coming to visit. If a cat is neutered and the pan is kept clean, there will be no unpleasant smell. Smell is inevitable with an unaltered cat in an apartment but, for a variety of reasons, I think it is madness to try to keep an unaltered cat in the city.

The amount of exercise a city cat gets and whether it ever sees the out-of-doors usually is determined by its temperament, its owner's inclinations, and the immediate surroundings. People in the city who have back yards often can let their cats roam in them. If the cat is altered it is not likely to stray. Failing a back yard, some people train their cats to collar and leash and take them for a daily constitutional. This is a fine practice, provided the cat likes it and the owner has time. Usually this training has to be started with a young kitten to be successful. If a cat firmly resists walking on a leash, don't try to force the issue. However, the danger of a cat's picking up germs on city streets is a vastly overrated one. Doubtless it picks up just as many germs in the apartment, brought in on people's clothes and shoes.

People who go to work every day may worry, when they first acquire a cat, about its being lonely. Actually, cats seem able to bear solitude much better than dogs. There are some pastimes that they enjoy a great deal, though, and it is nice to provide these for a solitary cat.

Minnie can amuse herself for hours with a dripping

faucet. I don't leave the water running, just keep forgetting to have a new washer put in the bathtub tap, so there is always a slow drop-drop for her to watch and pounce on and pat gently with one paw. Ping-pong balls are popular with almost all cats; so is cellophane. Small rubber balls or balls of tinfoil hanging on a string in a doorway are fun to bat back and forth. Every well-loved cat deserves a new catnip mouse about once a month. Best of all, probably, are paper bags. Cats dote on getting into paper bags, and in our household Thursday evening when I bring home the week's groceries is a red-letter day. Bags galore to scramble around in. However, games with string, thread, or fabric raveling should be forbidden. Too many cats swallow string and threaded needles and get into serious trouble. Television is endlessly fascinating to some cats. A friend of mine leaves her set on for her cat whenever she has to leave it alone.

Anyone who loves his cat better than his friends can always keep it entertained by asking an aleurophobe over for dinner once in a while. Cats have an uncanny way of spotting human cat-haters and enjoy jumping onto their laps.

The very nicest thing you can do for your cat is let it help you wrap packages. Cats love birthdays and Christmas and are indefatigable little hindrances in processes involving paper and ribbon. At Christmas we usually let Minnie help with a dummy package and do the more important ones after she has gone to bed.

Happily, there aren't many ways a cat can get into trouble or hurt itself in an apartment. But the greatest danger, falling out a window, is one many people fail to take into account, possibly because they believe the old saw about cats always landing on their feet. Cats do fall out of windows and out of trees and off roofs, and they do not always land on their feet. They may break bones, suffer internal injuries or be killed by the fall. Unless a window is on the ground floor or opens onto a fire escape it should be screened. The fact that cats do not have any mysterious wisdom concerning high places was borne in upon me young. We lived in a penthouse apartment and our cat, Curiosity, was very fond of ambling along the top of the wall that bordered the terrace. I was playing on the terrace one winter morning when a sudden movement made me look up. Curiosity had somehow miscalculated; his hind feet had slipped over the wall and all that I could see was the top of his head and two front paws clinging desperately to the bricks. The rest of him was dangling sixteen stories above the street. I was too frightened myself to move, which was probably just as well, and watched in horror as Curiosity slowly and painfully pulled himself back up. He did not take his daily stroll on the wall again after that.

Clothes dryers are a modern peril made to order for cats. Felines are curious, they like warmth and they like getting into things. If you don't want to find yourself with a fluff-dried cat some day, always make sure there is nothing more than the laundry inside when you turn the dryer on.

For country cats, automobiles are the greatest hazard. I am continually amazed and appalled by the number of motorists who seem to feel that if it's neither human nor a machine it's all right to hit it. Some cats seem to grasp instinctively the dangers inherent in fast-moving vehicles; others never do. There is not very much an owner can do about it except hope that his cat belongs to the first group.

Dogs are the next biggest menace to cats in the country. Some seem to chase them only for the fun of seeing them run; others pursue with intent to kill. Anyone who owns cats has a right to insist that the owners of cat-killing dogs keep them on their own property or adjust letting-out times with your cats. The cats are not likely to trespass.

Cats versus birds and the pros and cons of bells and collars are always good for heated debate among cat people—not to mention bird people. Like many cat owners, I am in the unhappy position of having a foot in both camps. I hate to see birds killed, but I haven't yet been able to devise any way to stop it. Some cats never try to catch birds; others try and never succeed. I once knew a cat that spent a great deal of her time stalking birds with such a signal lack of success that she became quite neurotic about them. Whenever she saw a bird she began to tremble and chatter angrily, as though she knew from the outset that she was bested. However, when a cat is both adept and determined, there is virtually nothing that can be done to protect the birds. Bells are, in my opinion, as good as useless. Minnie can walk upstairs with her bell on and never make a tinkle. Although the danger of a collar for country cats is frequently mentioned, none of my cats has ever gotten itself hung up by its collar. I do make sure, though, that the collar fits correctly.

Cat doors are not an essential in the country, but they save a great deal of jumping up and down to open doors, particularly when the cat is one that has trouble making up its mind about whether it wants to be in or out. Ready-made cat doors are sold for twenty dollars and up, but it is simpler and much less expensive to improvise one at home. Even if one hasn't the tools or the talent, a local handyman usually charges considerably less than twenty dollars to do the job. One cat door that I used in a city apartment was simply a wooden window box from the ten cent store. It lay upside down on the window sill with one opening cut into the side facing the room and another near the opposite end of the box, cut into the side facing outdoors. The window was left open just enough to accommodate the box which fitted snugly into the embrasure, and since the cat doors were at opposite ends, there was no draft. Another variety of homemade cat door that can be fitted into a window, or a hole cut in a door, consists of overlapping sections of stiff plastic, arranged in the same fashion as the shutter of a camera. They give easily against the pressure of the cat's body and keep out drafts the rest of the time.

There are many pleasures available to a country cat that a city one will never taste. Some cats like going for walks with their owners, and I am always delighted when one of mine does. If the cat has a sense of drama it can turn a ramble in the woods into an exciting adventure. I do not like ice skating myself, but my sister does, and when Minnie was younger she was very fond of accompanying her in this sport. She always skidded onto the ice with the same rather foolish expression of astonishment, and then slipped and slid along enthusiastically in the wake of the skaters. Most cats take an active interest in kite-flying. All the human members of my family do too, so many Sunday afternoons are happily spent in this pursuit.

It is a rare cat that doesn't like to garden. My feelings about this are mixed, since cats do not approach the work with quite the same aims that I do. They like to help dig the hole, which is fine, but they like even better to scratch the seeds out of the holes as soon as you have finished putting them in. They also enjoy lying on the few seedlings that have escaped to come up. I'm afraid cats and serious gardening are not really very compatible, but I have never been able to persuade a cat of this.

Feline reactions to travel vary enormously with the individual and range from vast enjoyment to stark terror. But in all cases cats are likely to view traveling with more enthusiasm if they become accustomed to it while they are young and if nothing frightening happens to them on the first outing. Even if you don't anticipate making any long trips with a cat, it is wise to get it used to driving as a kitten so that if later it is necessary to transport it to the vet or a boarding kennel there will be no unnecessary panic or difficulty connected with the journey.

For long trips with cats, cars are infinitely preferable to any other means of transportation. If the cat is used to being in a car, it needn't stay in a container. Usually it likes to stretch out on the shelf under the rear window.

Like dogs, cats travel best on an empty stomach, and shouldn't be fed for four or five hours before setting out. On a trip of up to eighteen or twenty hours, they needn't be fed en route, either; when feeding is necessary, half portions are recommended. Water, though, should always be available.

If driving seems to excite a cat a greal deal or make it feel queasy, it can be given a tranquilizer half an hour before starting. A fifty milligram dramamine, available without prescription, will usually work well; if it doesn't, ask a vet to prescribe something else. Any tranquilizer should be pretested, before the trip starts. Some cats react to them the way some infants react to sedatives—they get hopped up instead of calmed down.

Provided the cat has no violent objection to collar and leash, it is a good idea to have it wear them while traveling. They are a safeguard against a frightened cat bolting, and also make exercising possible on a long journey.

The simplest way to deal with toilet arrangements is to carry the cat's pan in the back of the car if there is room. One of our cats refused to use the pan in the car, but when it said it had to go we stopped, put the pan down beside the road and the cat obligingly hopped in, performed and jumped back into the car. I wish my children were as co-operative.

The rules concerning animals on trains and planes differ, depending on the line; it is always best to check beforehand. To ensure being able to keep a cat in the passenger section of a train, one usually has to reserve a compartment, though sometimes a lenient conductor will overlook a cat in the coaches, provided it is in a container.

If a cat has to be shipped—a harrowing experience at best—air freight is by far the best way. For shipping, a cat needs a comfortable container, one that will protect it from drafts, be large enough to turn around in and to accommodate a toilet pan. There must be a water dish in the container, of course, but unless the trip is to last several days, the cat will do better without food. If you want it to be fed en route, you will, of course, have to send food along with it.

The welcome extended to cats by hotels and motels varies, depending on management policies. I think it is wise to inquire ahead of time, if possible. Trying to sneak a cat in can lead to problems. The Gaines Dog Research Center at 250 Park Avenue, New York City, publishes a most helpful pamphlet called "Touring With Towser," which lists hotels and motels across the country in which guests may be accompanied by dogs. It is available to the public on request, and I trust I am not being chauvinistic when I say I feel sure that any place Towser can get in, Minnie can too.

Chapter III

Of Mice and Menus

For thousands of years before scientific study of nutrition was initiated, the human race nevertheless managed to nourish itself with varying degrees of adequacy. So, for thousands of years, has the domestic cat. Like humans, cats are marvelously adaptable creatures, capable of surviving, if not always thriving, on whatever is at hand. As a child I raised litters and litters of kittens. I realize now I didn't feed them properly, yet most of them grew into apparently healthy and happy cats. This would seem to confirm the "Shucks, cats can get along on anything" line of reasoning, but, in fact, it does nothing of the sort. In the first place, my kittens were barn kittens with opportunities to forage for things I failed to give them. Secondly, I'm sure that had my kittens been weighed, measured, x-rayed and their life spans recorded, it

41

would have been discovered that poor nutrition had had results invisible to the naked eye: slightly rickety bones, perhaps, smaller stature or lower disease resistance. The cat can indeed get along on an imperfect diet—millions of them do—but people who own and love cats usually hope to do better than that by them.

However, when the cat owner sets out to discover the best of all possible diets for his pet, he is apt to find himself mired in controversy, outright contradiction or utter confusion. Feline nutrition is an infant science, and understandably so. Laboratory studies of the exact food requirements of an animal are expensive and usually are not undertaken unless the animal is one whose habits give clues to human nutrition, or like cows or chickens its diet is of major economic importance. Unhappily, there have not been these spurs to the study of feline nutrition and so the number of facts we can accept as unquestionable is few indeed. The questions to which we do not yet have answers are myriad.

It is for this reason that veterinarians, from long practical experience, usually advise that a cat be fed a variety of foods. No one has, at this writing, definitely proved exactly how much of certain elements—minerals and fats, for instance— are essential to the cat. The only safe way to hedge the bet is to offer such a varied diet that the chances of completely omitting some vital element are reduced.

This may seem confusing to those who assume that since cats are carnivores their normal diet would be meat. Just meat. It is true that mammals are divided into three groups— carnivores, herbivores and omnivores—on the bases of what they eat and their equipment for so doing. The domestic cat has indeed the typical eating equipment of a carnivore: sharp, flesh-tearing teeth rather than flat-surfaced, grain-grinding teeth, and short, typically carnivorous intestines, not designed, as are those of the herbivore, for the slow digestion of vegetable matter. But its diet is atypical. In a natural state cats eat meat: mice and other rodents, birds, fish and insects. But they also eat grasses, ferns, herbs and the vegetable contents of their prey's stomach.

If you consider this for a moment you realize that a cat feeding itself does just what veterinarians advise you to do for it; from a seemingly small selection of available foods, it provides itself with considerable nutritional variety. Shuddery as it may be to contemplate, reflect that one entire mouse (and they are consumed entire) represents flesh, muscle, bone, organs and pre-digested vegetable matter— each contributing different vital elements. It may be unappetizing to humans, but it is sound.

The lesson to be learned from this is not that a cat owner has to turn mousenapper to keep his pet healthy, nor that all human food is unfit for cat consumption. The lesson is simply that cats cannot live by flesh alone. A cat that is given just one thing, day in and day out, year after year, is inevitably going to suffer from a nutritional deficiency sooner or later. And it is my conviction that this axiom applies to most prepared pet foods, as well as to fresh foods, no matter what it says on the label about percentages of this and that.

All cats, it is agreed, need the following elements: proteins (which are composed of a number of different amino acids and are essential to life), minerals, fats, some of the vitamins, and water. How do you translate these abstract-sounding terms into foods? Probably there are as many ways of presenting the essentials as there are cats, and they can be as simple or as dressy as the cat owner's fancy or convenience dictates. However, in general, it can be said that a diet which includes muscle meats and organ meats, fish, eggs, milk (if it agrees with the cat, and it doesn't invariably), some vegetables and water will feed a grown cat adequately.

To be more explicit, here are some of the more ordinary foods in which the essential elements may be found:

Proteins: egg, muscle meat, organ meat, milk, cottage cheese.

Fats: meat, butter, cheese, whole milk, cream, some fish, some vegetables.

Minerals: milk, meat, fish, egg, organs, bone meal, some of the vegetables.

Vitamins A, B complex, D, E: milk, egg, fish liver, glandular organs, yellow and green vegetables, whole wheat, cereals, fats. (It appears that cats make their own vitamin C and do not require vitamin K.)

Water: food is one source, of course; muscle meat, for instance, may be 75 per cent moisture. However, don't forget that all cats need drinking water too—some a great deal, some a small amount—and a dish should always be available.

You may have noticed that carbohydrates, essential to human nutrition, haven't been mentioned. This brings up the great old mashed potato controversy. For many years it was believed that cats not only didn't need carbohydrates, but that starchy foods actually made them ill. Potatoes, macaroni, spaghetti, noodles, bread, cake, baked beans are just some of the starches we were told never to feed a cat. Laboratory studies have changed this view. They show that while cats have no specific need for carbohydrate, they can utilize its calories, and that starchy foods make a perfectly acceptable filler, provided they don't displace the essential fats and proteins.

It is the construction of the cat's gut which has given rise to this misconception about starches. Felines have extremely short intestines, even for carnivores, and consequently are not able to deal with the cellulose coatings of some of the starchy foods. Corn kernels, peas, dried beans and so forth are simply not digested; they emerge exactly as they entered. However, if they are cooked and mashed, to break open the coating, the cat can digest them perfectly well.

Meanwhile, there sits your cat, looking expectant, and what are you going to feed it?

This brings us to the matter of prepared pet foods. The notion has been carefully built up in the mind of the public, by labeling and advertising, that all one has to do to provide puss with an absolutely yummy, highly nutritious diet is to go to the cupboard and open a can of Brand X. That is my principal objection to prepared foods as such—the idea that they can be the whole answer to proper diet. Perhaps one day, when we know all there is to know about the cat's needs, such an answer may come in cans. But right now it does not, and any cat that is fed exclusively on commercial pet food may be courting deficiencies—to a greater or lesser extent, depending on the quality of the food. Aside from the lack of variety of a prepared-food-and-nothing-else diet, there are certain pitfalls in some of the foods themselves. Some brands, for instance, may contain such a high proportion of water that there is almost no nourishment of any kind in them. Most of the canned fish foods for cats are made of whole fish, ground up—the advertising boasting that thus kitty is getting all the rich nutritional elements a fish can provide. It may indeed be getting a lot of rich, nutritional elements—and possibly in entirely wrong proportions. Once, after I had opened a can of cat fish, it was somehow allowed to sit on the window sill for a week. When I rediscovered the can all the moisture had evaporated. I was considerably taken aback to see that it now contained nothing but a heap of pulverized bones; rather a small heap, at that.

Although there may be disagreement about exact percentages, nutritional research on cats has demonstrated quite conclusively that they thrive best on a diet high in protein and fat. Here is another area where the commercial foods are likely to be found wanting. They may provide adequate protein, but often do not provide adequate fats. A recent study at Harvard shows a relationship between the amount of fat in the diet and the absorption of vitamin A by cats. A cat that does not get enough fat may not get enough vitamin A, and this deficiency can lead to a variety of ills.

This is not meant to damn forever all commercial pet foods. Obviously, if you are feeding a large number of cats, canned food is the most practical solution—supplemented, of course, by other things. However, canned foods should be approached with caution. Don't choose simply on the basis of economy. Don't use one brand exclusively. Don't give it and nothing else. Your veterinarian will probably be glad to tell you the brands he has found most satisfactory and how to supplement them.

The question of what kind of meat to feed a cat is surrounded by such a formidable batch of misconceptions that it can seem extremely difficult and extremely expensive to serve a cat a decent meal. We used to be told that cats should have only lean meat. Cats, we now know, need fat. The optimum amount is not known but lies somewhere between 5 per cent and 25 per cent of their diet. Meat is a good source, so the cheaper, fatty cuts of meats are fine. We also used to hear that only beef, veal, lamb and chicken were suitable. Not so. Pork is a perfectly good meat. So is horse meat, and it is the cheapest of all. While liver is probably the highest quality protein available, cats find the cheaper, nourishing organs like kidney, heart and lung quite delectable as alternates.

Table scraps are often sneered at as being greasy, over-spiced, unwholesome plate scrapings, fit only for pigs or the garbage pail, never for a cat. I do not agree, and neither do most of the experts. A recent manual on the care of laboratory animals says, in its section on cats: "Scraps from a hospital kitchen (after being well cooked) may form part of the diet." Certainly among those little dishes of leftovers that populate every refrigerator there are bound to be some things which do very nicely to round out a cat's meal. What about meat scraps? Or a dab of this or that vegetable, a bit of cooked cereal or egg, a smidgen of cottage cheese? These are all wholesome foods, and the fact that they were prepared originally for people, not cats, doesn't detract from their wholesomeness.

In the literature about cats, the dietary don'ts are legion, and most of them are unnecessary. I say unnecessary because you would have to work pretty long and hard to make a cat fall in love with a food that was really bad for it. Something very highly spiced—a curry, for instance—would undoubtedly disagree with a cat. But first you would have to persuade the cat to eat it. And among other foods sternly prohibited—frankfurters, alligator pears, bananas, porridge, to choose at random—there's no evidence that an occasional small amount of any would do the slightest harm. Obviously a diet composed exclusively of any one such food would be likely to do a cat in eventually—or even a human, for that matter. More sensible dietary don'ts are those tailored to the highly individual digestive system of your own cat. Some cats get diarrhea from milk, for instance, or from egg or liver. Experience will show you what to leave off the menu. A more complex problem, because so little still is known about it, is allergy. Unfortunately cats can have allergies, a fact that has rather recently come to light. When a cat is allergic to certain foods, the sensitivity often manifests itself in an eczema. If you have this sort of problem you will undoubtedly need your vet's help in pinpointing it.

Just as cats' digestive systems are widely individual, so, too, are their tastes. I have known those who adored grapes, potato chips, petunia leaves and cassava melon. Minnie's idea of heaven is leftover salad with French dressing. If a cat's basic diet is sound, I see no reason why it shouldn't indulge occasionally in these supplementary goodies—and there may be something it really needs in these treats.

This brings us to catnip, which gives such joy to so many cats. Strictly speaking, this herb is not a food—only occasional cats eat the leaves—but it is definitely a treat. In the country I grow it in our herb bed; city dwellers can always find catnip-stuffed toys at pet shops.

There are innumerable ways, plain and fancy, of presenting the dietary essentials to a cat. Those who enjoy toiling in a hot kitchen are welcome to the fancy ways. Personally, I prefer the simple, and I think I'm doing my pets as well as myself a favor. Cats are not gourmets, but they are creatures of very strong habit; it is easy for them to become used, almost addicted, to a certain food or method of preparation, and remarkably hard for their owners to persuade them to change their ways.

Scientific opinion is that cats choose food more on the basis of smell than of any other factor. Strong smell equals good food in a cat's book. Good food may come to mean best food and then, often, the only food that it will consider. For this reason, I never serve such strong-smelling delicacies as liver, kidney or fish alone, but mix them in so thoroughly with the rest of the meal that the cat has no opportunity to decide that the delicacy alone is all it wants to eat. This is what veterinarians call a bland, blended ration. Since no strong smell predominates, the blend can be varied from day to day to provide the necessary balance of diet without upsetting the cat's expectations. Those of my cats that I've managed to keep in happy ignorance that such a thing as pure liver exists think it is just as delicious in a blend. Unlike people, cats do not mind monotony in tastes; in fact, they prefer it.

The pros and cons of cooked versus raw meat are more complicated to sort out. It is safe to say that some of the nutritive values may be lost in cooking; however, it is often more convenient to feed cooked meat. Unlike dogs, who are firm believers in the riper the better, cats do not like meat that is spoiling. Raw meat does not keep well, unless it is frozen, and therefore can entail a good many more trips to the butcher. I usually compromise by varying raw with cooked meat to suit my own convenience. Two meats which should not be fed raw are rabbit and fresh-water fish. Either may harbor a particular variety of tapeworm which is transmissible to the cat unless killed by cooking. We are usually warned, too, against raw pork because of the danger of trichinosis. This is a possible but, so far as I have been able to discover, unproven danger for cats. However, it is probably just as well to play it safe by cooking pork before feeding it.

Certainly the neatest way to feed cats, who enjoy dragging large chunks around, is to mince their food. It is not the best way for the cat, unhappily. Although cavities are virtually unknown in feline teeth, years of soft diet with no opportunities for exercising the gums almost always produce the same problems they do in humans—deposits of tartar, reddened, sensitive gums, and, eventually, loose teeth. To keep their mouths healthy, cats need to gnaw on something to exercise their gums, so every once in a while it is a good idea to present them with a large bone with some meat left on it, or sizable chunks of raw muscle meat.

Anyone who has ever heard anything about dogs and cats has heard of the danger of letting them eat bones that may splinter. The danger of fish bones is a very real one for cats. Except in the case of canned fish where the bones have been processed to a crumbly consistency, fish must always be boned before it is fed. The small, needlelike bones are very likely to lodge somewhere or to puncture something. The perils of chicken and chop bones are considerably less for cats than for dogs. However, there can always be a first time, and it is just as well to avoid them.

Something that cats without execption are extremely particular about is the temperature of their food. They dislike intensely food that is icy cold. Both liquid and solid foods should be served at room temperature. And, because it is a creature of habit, your cat will appreciate being fed at roughly the same times each day, and in the same place. I've even known cats that felt strongly about having food served in a particular dish, as well. If you have more than one cat, feed them from separate dishes. Mealtimes seem to be more relaxed for everyone that way.

How many meals a cat needs a day and how many it gets are two very different things. Theoretically, one meal a day is enough for a grown cat that is neither pregnant nor nursing. Few cats will let you get away with anything as mere as that. On my veterinarian's recommendation, I have settled on a morning and evening meal, with a saucer of milk in between, to everyone's apparent satisfaction. However, this vet wryly adds that every time he goes into his own kitchen, his wife seems to be feeding the cats. So, really, the factors to weigh in this matter are the cat's contentment and your own convenience, or devotion.

Because there is this wide latitude in how often a cat may

be fed, it is a mistake to think there may safely be the same latitude in how much it is fed in a day. It is possible to underfeed cats, to overfeed, and to misfeed cats—by assuming that quantity is a substitute for quality or that large amounts of the wrong things will nourish them as adequately as smaller amounts of the proper foods. Cats are more frequently misfed than underfed, although the results are outwardly the same: they look and act hungry all the time. Most frequently of all they are overfed.

There are so many factors involved in determining the proper daily ration for a grown cat that it is almost impossible to give any hard and fast rule. Weight and size are the most obvious, of course, but the cat's environment, the amount of exercise it gets, its temperament—whether placid or highstrung—and its age all affect the amount of food it needs. There have been studies made on the caloric requirements of cats that are enlightening to the nutritionist, but not of great practical help to the average cat owner who has neither the time nor the knowledge to compute calories exactly. However, a simplified translation of the findings would be: a mature cat, weighing between ten and twelve pounds, needs between 250 and 400 calories daily. There are between 500 and 800 calories to a pound in a mixed ration containing the necessary nutritional elements—proteins, fats, vitamins, minerals, and carbohydrate filler. Therefore, about half a pound of this ration, split into x number of feedings, should keep your cat lean and hard—which is what you are aiming for.

Many people overfeed cats because they believe the old saw that cats, unlike dogs, know when they have had enough. Well, they don't. Almost any animal, including the human, will eat more than it needs if the meal is appetizing. It is not doing the cat a favor to allow it to overeat. Fat cats, we now know, are heir to many of the ills that beset overweight people, including a shortened life expectancy.

How can you tell if a cat is too fat? Unfortunately you can't use that index so infallible for humans: the skirt or trousers that suddenly gap at the waist. Furthermore, a cat's coat is a camouflage that makes chubbiness hard to detect. But there are ways. Run your hands over its sides; there should not be a pad of fat between your fingers and the ribs. Turn puss on its back and feel the insides of its hind legs; if there are large, pendulous pockets of fat there, the cat is overweight. This is not likely to happen to a growing cat, but any time after the second year, particularly to a city cat, overweight is an ever-present menace.

Reducing a cat is no cinch; the cat sees to that. They are old hands at making people feel like dogs. Your pet will be quick to notice that you have cut down its portions, and the reproaches will be constant and piteous. It takes character to withstand the unblinking eye fixed on you every time you put a bite into your own mouth, the mournful twinings around your ankles whenever you approach the vicinity of the refrigerator, the loud demands for just a mouthful of this or that. But you must withstand. You are not a cat-starver, a sadist, a heartless wretch, as your plump little pal would like to make you believe. Remember that this imploring creature could actually live on nothing more than its own fat and water for a surprising length of time. The feeding rules you follow are those of a sensible reducing diet for humans: reduce the total intake, slowly but inexorably, while you cut the carbohydrates to a minimum, keep the fat content low and the protein high. When you can feel pussy's rib cage distinctly once again you have arrived at the proper daily portion.

When a cat is finicky about food, somebody or something made it that way. The something might be an allergy, but more often the cause is somebody who allowed it to become habituated to a certain food or foods. With a young kitten this problem can be avoided by feeding it a bland, blended ration. Even with a grown cat with built-in food prejudices, all is not lost. The stern but perfectly legitimate method of letting it go without until it is hungry enough to eat whatever is offered will usually do the trick in a few days. Occasionally, you run into a cat whose will power is stronger than yours. My veterinarian bitterly recalls a particular Siamese which he once boarded for a month. It so resented being where it was that it adamantly refused anything and everything it was offered, no matter how he petted, pleaded and cajoled. It was perfectly well-disposed toward him, but it was on a hunger strike. Finally he had to resort to intravenous feeding and believes if he hadn't and if the cat's owner had left it there much longer, it would literally have starved itself to death. Incidentally, the owner reported that once the Siamese got home it embarked on an eating binge of staggering proportions, and where it had once been frightfully fussy about what it would and wouldn't taste, it now fell eagerly upon anything she offered. I doubt that many cats are this determined, but if you have not triumphed in the battle of wills in a few days, at most a week, there is a subtler method of changing the cat's mind about its food. This plays on the fact that a cat, like a person, can stand almost anything if it is introduced gradually. By this method, you sneak up on the cat, blending a bit of the new feed into its ration every day and withdrawing a bit of the old, until you have achieved the new diet.

The finicky cat is not to be confused with a cat that suddenly refuses its ordinary food. In this case, it may be full, sick, have a toothache, or a foreign body lodged in its mouth or throat. If the reason isn't readily apparent, let it skip that day's meal. By the following day, its behavior should give you a clue to the cause. If the cat greets the food eagerly, then doesn't touch it, the trouble is probably in its mouth. If it has fever, diarrhea, constipation, or vomits, the trouble is internal. In any case, if your cat refuses food for twenty-four hours, it should be seen by a vet. (See Chapter VII.)

Some cats vomit very easily. There are several possible causes for this. One, which it would take a vet to diagnose, might be a congenital defect. Another is allergy. If the cat always vomits after eating a certain food, such as egg or milk, the chances are it is sensitive to that food. See if omitting it from the diet solves the problem. Perfectly healthy young cats have a tendency to overeat or to gobble and promptly throw up. This can usually be obviated by feeding three or four small meals a day.

An obvious candidate for an increased number of meals is the pregnant or the nursing cat. The gestation period is roughly nine weeks, and at about the fifth week the mother begins to need more nourishment to compensate for what the kittens are taking. She will probably be quite frank about letting you know this, but whether she is or not, you should increase her intake somewhat. This might be done by offering her three meals, each just a little smaller than the two she is accustomed to, plus an increased amount of milk if she is a milk drinker. The quality of her diet is particularly important at this time, too, especially as far as protein goes. Liver is high quality protein while gelatin, which is extracted from bones, is low quality. To cover any possible dietary gaps, veterinarians often recommend multiple-vitamin drops like Tri-Vi-Sol or Abdec, 0.3 c.c. mixed in the daily ration. Though vets are not as stern as obstetricians about weight-gaining in pregnancy, they don't like to see a pregnant cat become grossly fat, simply because it is likely to make the birth of the kittens more difficult. The ideal while the female is carrying and nursing kittens is to give her enough to maintain her and the kittens adequately, but not so much that she turns into a tub of lard.

For the first weeks of her kittens' lives, the mother takes entire and efficient care of them (see Chapter IV for details). However, when their milk teeth begin to break through, somewhere between three and four weeks, it is time for you to lend a hand with their feeding. Ordinarily, weaning is a gratifyingly simple affair if you go about it methodically.

The first food to introduce is milk. There used to be a theory that only goat's milk would do. After that went out of fashion, cow's milk was considered acceptable. Now most vets agree that evaporated milk diluted half and half with water is less likely to cause diarrhea, one of the major problems of weaning. It should be offered at room temperature in small amounts several times daily. Of course, you will have to get across to the kittens that this milk is to be lapped, not sucked, but that is usually easy. Often they make this discovery for themselves. If one fails to, put a small, shallow saucer of milk down in front of the kitten, then dip your finger in the milk and rub it against the kitten's mouth. It will lick its mouth. Dip your finger again and hold it up to be licked, urging the kitten to the saucer itself by leaving your finger closer to it each time you dip. Most kittens get the idea very fast, especially if you introduce the saucer for the first time when they have not nursed for several hours. This method is preferable to the rough-and-ready one of pushing the kitten's nose into the milk, which is like teaching a child to swim by throwing him in the water.

Meat is usually next on the weaning agenda, and the

strained baby meats are ideal for this purpose. How soon you start on it depends on the kittens. If the milk seems to be causing diarrhea, try cutting it out and going straight to strained meat. Then go on to the junior meats and then ordinary meat minced fairly fine. When kittens are doing well on evaporated milk, you may mix soft-boiled egg or raw egg yolk into their formula. Egg white should not be used raw, since it may prevent the absorption of certain vitamins. One egg, mixed into a two-day supply of formula, is enough for four kittens, so you can work up or down from there, depending on the size of your litter. A rule of thumb to follow on amounts is, roughly: about an ounce of food per day at one month (if the kittens are still nursing and usually they are until the fifth to seventh week), two ounces at two months, three ounces at three. The rate of increase slows down slightly at about four months. To break these amounts down into proportions, the preferred daily ration is: two parts beef to one part milk and one part cooked egg. A kitten on this diet is getting a good start in life.

Hand-raising kittens from birth is another, and considerably trickier matter. But if you're a game, or just a desperate, foster parent, you will find the techniques discussed in Chapter IV.

It seems incredible that so many ancient superstitions connected with cat feeding persist. These hoary myths are like the indestructible targets in shooting galleries. Time and again they're riddled with holes, only to bob up again for the next customer.

Probably the most venerable legend is that raw meat makes cats vicious. Countless owners have dutifully stewed up pussy's food for the sake of pussy's disposition and thereby wasted valuable time and probably even more valuable food elements. Because this is utter nonsense.

When we knew even less than we do now about the skin ailments of cats and their causes, a theory was developed that certain foods were responsible. They were "heatening to the blood," the legend ran, and made it "boil out," rather like an automobile radiator, in skin rashes of one kind or another. The fact that when a cat's skin is inflamed it feels hot to the touch may be partly responsible for this theory. Actually, of course, no food can change the temperature of the blood, and the commoner skin ailments of cats are known to be caused by fungi or external parasites. Endocrine imbalance and food allergy are more infrequent causes.

The meanest myth of all is that a cat kept as a mouser should never be fed or it would neglect its work. The owner who follows this advice succeeds only in starving the cat or making it think of looking around for a better home.

A misguided belief, perpetuated by many pet shops, is that cats need supplementary sulphur in the form of pellets or tonics added to their food or drinking water. The truth is that cats are unable to absorb sulphur in this form and, anyway, are probably getting all they need—in a form they can absorb—in their diet. Lime water, too, has long been touted as a diet supplement that helps neutralize acidity and prevent diarrhea. It neutralizes the acidity, all right, but this is not a desirable thing to do. The cat needs all the stomach acids it has, to digest its food.

And, finally, if anyone tells you that milk makes worms, don't believe it. Worms make worms.

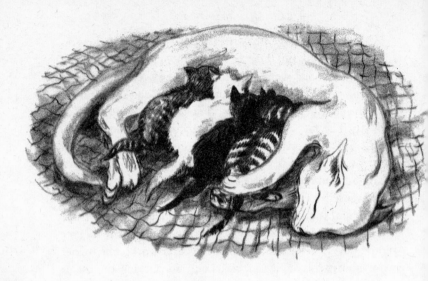

Chapter IV

Love and Consequences

Even people who have never owned cats usually know all too well what a cat's sex life sounds like. The calling and squalling, hissing and yowling that rend the night air are unmistakable and alarming sounds. In a way, it is fitting they should be. Cats, both toms and females, take sex with a deadly seriousness. A female cat in season is preoccupied with the necessity for mating to the exclusion of almost every other interest, as her behavior makes embarrassingly evident to squeamish people, and toms will fight each other for her favor with unbelievable ferocity.

Less well known are the mechanics of feline reproduction. Toms usually reach sexual maturity at around nine months. Females ordinarily come in season for the first time at about

58

six months. It is known that the length of the days influences the onset of the mating cycles in all animals—light stimulating the pituitary gland—and the periods of estrus for cats are usually summer, when days are longest, and January, when the days once again begin to grow longer. But there are many females who seem not to play by the rules, or whose pituitary glands are confused by artificial light, and they may come into season at any time or even manage to squeeze in three litters a year. Unlike dogs, female cats come in season repeatedly during their two annual heat periods unless they are mated, which stops the cycles. The female's timetable may go like this: in season for four or five days and receptive to males; if not mated, a dormant period of eighteen to twenty days follows; then another receptive period followed by another dormant period, followed by another receptive period. There may be as many as four or more of these five-day periods with dormant periods in between, all of which means that the female's period of sexual interest occupies an awful lot of her time.

There is a simple physiological explanation for this behavior of female cats. Unlike dogs, they ordinarily do not ovulate until they are mated. During the days when the female is receptive to males, the lining of the ovary is covered with countless blisterlike follicles, each containing an egg. These follicles, however, do not rupture to release their eggs until the cat is mated. (This, of course, is one reason cats almost never fail to conceive; it is practically impossible for the egg and sperm to miss each other.) If the cat is not mated, the eggs are resorbed and the dormant period follows while a new batch of eggs is developing. As soon as ovulation occurs, substances called luteal bodies form in the follicles, secreting a hormone that puts an end to mating behavior. Apparently the action of the pituitary gland is somewhat like an electric charge which gradually loses its force, so that even in unmated cats, the development of eggs gradually peters out and the estrus cycle ends.

I had always assumed that no one could fail to notice when a female cat was in season. Her very explicit postures, her spine-tingling calls and her singleminded determination to get out and find a tom would seem to make it abundantly clear. However, my vet tells me my assumption is incorrect, and told me of a lady sitting in her living room having a quiet talk with the family doctor when her young cat began to take on most strangely. The lady was alarmed, as was the doctor, who suggested that the cat appeared to have gone out of its head. A hasty call was made to the vet who rushed to the house and after a quick look pronounced the cat to be in heat. The doctor, needless to say, was even more shamefaced than the lady. However, cats do not signal their condition with any amount of discharge—their aggressive behavior seems to take its place in courting—so there is not, fortunately, the problem of spots on furniture and carpets that there is with bitches in season.

Toms, like females, have a physiological idiosyncracy that apparently plays an important role in reproduction. The penis of males is covered with small, sharp barbs. It is believed that their purpose is to insure ovulation in the female by increased stimulation. It is also thought that the pain caused by the withdrawal of the barbs is what produces the female's hair-raising cry.

Anyone interested in breeding cats should have some notion of what feline mating behavior is usually like. Here is a clear and accurate description from a scientific paper:

"As the male begins to approach the female, he issues a characteristically short, chirp-like sex call. An experienced receptive female usually responds . . . by assuming a crouching stance. The male runs toward the female and grabs the loose skin on the back of her neck in his mouth. This neck grip tends to immobilize the female, enabling the male to mount her. He does so by placing his forepaws against her sides, a few inches behind her forelegs. Within a few seconds, the male places his hind legs over the female's hind region so that the male's body now lies directly above and parallel to the body of the female. The female bends her back . . . with her . . . forearms lying flat on the floor. The male soon begins to rub the flanks of the female with his forepaws and at the same time starts a stepping movement with his hind legs, raising first one and then the other, and swaying sideways. . . . At this time the female begins to tread by pushing against the floor with her hind legs, and with her tail bent sharply to one side. . . . The male then begins a series of vigorous pelvic thrusts . . . (there is) a loud . . . cry from the female as the male executes a terminal lunge. . . . After about ten seconds, the female turns sharply on the male, hissing and pawing, and throws him off her back."*

This behavior is followed by a short period of extremely absorbed licking and rolling by the female, who will then go on and do the whole thing all over again if there are more willing toms around. It is quite possible that of the resulting litter each kitten may have been sired by a different tom.

There is a possibility that carrying a litter of kittens may slightly stunt the growth of an immature cat, and ideally females would not be allowed to breed until their second period of estrus, when they have achieved their full growth and strength. However, it is just about impossible to persuade them to wait this long, and most cats, on a good diet, are hardy enough to withstand the strains of pregnancy and

* By Jay S. Rosenblatt and Lester R. Aronson, *Behavior*, Vol. XII, 4, 1958.

birth. Any vet will say, however, that no female should be allowed to breed unless she is in good general health—free of skin disease, internal parasites or other debilitating ailments —and being fed a sound, varied diet. If a cat has ever been hit by a car, she should be x-rayed to make sure her pelvis was not fractured in the accident. A fractured pelvis is a common, and frequently undetected injury, and a female who has had one is very likely to die trying to give birth to her kittens, unless a Caesarean is performed. Without question, she should be spayed. Occasionally, as in a case like this, the owner may not discover that the cat shouldn't breed until it is too late to spay. Under these circumstances, a veterinarian may recommend a chemical abortion.

Many people seem to feel apologetic about having their pets neutered because, they say, it is wrong to rob an animal of its sexual potency. This strikes me as an unrealistic attitude. Planned parenthood is almost impossible to achieve in the feline world, and it seems far more wrong to allow thousands of kittens to be born that nobody wants. I also believe it is more humane to neuter a cat than to leave it intact but doomed to a life of celibacy—a neat trick if you can pull it off, and some determined cat-owners manage to.

From a purely practical and possibly selfish standpoint, the arguments for neutering cats kept as house pets, particularly in the city, are many. The female spends a large portion of her life in season and if she is not kept under lock and key, either at home or in a boarding kennel, during these periods, is capable of producing ten or more kittens a year— many more than any one person feels like being responsible for. It takes the vigilance of a platoon of jailers to keep her from finding a tom and the patience of Job to cope with the restlessness that her failure to find one produces. The most restrained female I ever owned nearly drove me mad when she was in heat, simply by sitting on the window sill all day long with her nose pressed to the pane, piteously calling, Hew*wo*? Hew*wo*? Hew-*wo*? And she was a model of maidenliness. Less modest females call loud and long, roll, climb, pace, overeat or starve, stop using their sand boxes and may even spray somewhat in the manner of a tom with sex on his mind. Altogether, they are not the best of companions at these times, particularly for children.

Almost every facet of a tom's sexual behavior presents a sound argument for altering, either in the cat's best interests or the owner's. Aesthetically speaking, an unaltered male does not make a very satisfactory house pet. Not only does his urine always have a characteristically strong, unpleasant, and virtually ineradicable smell, but it is practically impossible to keep him from spraying. This performance, alluring to female cats, but definitely not to human beings, consists of backing up to an object (such as a table leg, door or hanging garment) and urinating on it. This problem is not so acute if the cat is a country tom, but in a city apartment the presence of an unaltered male makes the premises well nigh uninhabitable by anyone who hasn't a very bad head cold.

Possibly, if cats could be sounded on the subject, they might say they would rather have a short happy life than a long celibate one. But I would not want to give the option to any cat of which I'm fond, and there is no doubt that altered males live longer than unaltered ones. Domestic toms may never kill each other in battle, but they certainly inflict terrible damage. Instinct makes them go unerringly for each other's heads and testicles, and both winner and loser may retire from the conflict with horrible wounds. The fighting of certain other animals is quite ritualistic, with no one really getting hurt. Rattlesnakes, for example, never strike at each other, but Indian wrestle to a decision. This most

63

definitely is not true of felines. And the bite of a cat is particularly toxic to another cat because the disease organisms in the biter's mouth find the perfect place in which to thrive in the victim's flesh. That is why abscesses so often develop from bite wounds, and abscesses are no joke. They can, among other things, eventually lead to liver abscesses and heart disease.

No matter how satisfied his expression, it is extremely distressing to have your cat come home with his coat in tatters and his ears chewed to shreds. Even more distressing, he may not come home at all. When, in my childhood, our barn cat, Socksie, was so regularly populating the countryside with kittens, I remember that as each litter grew up, the males just disappeared. I never knew whether they were killed or simply driven off by a more dominant tom, for there appears to be a boss cat in any feline colony. I remember too that when we moved to the city, we children were allowed to choose one young tom to take with us. For two months, Curiosity devoted all his cunning to the project of escaping from our sixteenth-floor apartment, while we devoted all ours to keeping him from escape. One day the back door was left open just a crack, and that was enough. In this case there is a happy ending because weeks later someone in the neighborhood recognized him and brought him back to us, very dirty, very hungry, and very much chewed up. He was altered promptly, and lived to a ripe and comfortable old age.

The argument most frequently advanced against neutering cats is that the operation is likely to have side effects, making them fat, lazy and uninteresting. There is no scientific proof whatsoever of this contention. Cats get fat when they are overfed and underexercised, and cats that are too fat are liable to be lazy. But no laboratory studies exist to prove conclusively that a properly-fed altered cat automatically becomes fat. It is quite true that altered toms may grow larger than they would have if left intact, because the male hormone, testosterone, which is no longer secreted after altering, is an inhibitor of growth. Size and weight, though, are certainly not synonymous. There is no evidence either that altered toms are socially unacceptable to other cats. An unaltered tom may exhibit some signs of bafflement at his first encounter with an altered one, but usually altered males have just as many friends as any other cat. After Curiosity's operation we moved from a top-floor apartment to a ground-floor one, and Curiosity usually made his evening entrances and exits through my bedroom window. I got quite used to waking up and finding not only Curiosity purring peacefully on the foot of my bed, but two or three of his pals from the alley as well. And, like spayed females, altered males make gentler, more playful and more reliable companions for people.

Cats may be neutered at any time in their lives, provided they are in normal good health and not so old that they can't withstand surgery. Veterinarians usually advise altering toms somewhere between seven and nine months, before they reach sexual maturity, and spaying females at about five months, before their first heat period. Contrary to popular belief, the fact that a cat has had one or more litters does not mean she cannot be spayed. In fact, spaying is often advised for a female that is rundown from bearing too many litters. Although it can be done, veterinarians do not like to spay a female that is in season, pregnant or nursing kittens.

The neutering of cats is done under anesthesia and, barring complications, is neither painful nor difficult. To alter a male, the testicles are removed, making him sterile. His interest in sex becomes just about nil, his urine no longer smells rank and he stops spraying. Spaying females involves removing the ovaries and uterus, a somewhat more extensive procedure, comparable to a hysterectomy. After spaying, the female stops coming in season.

There is a new oral contraceptive on the market now for dogs, and though it has not yet been released for cats, very likely it will be in the next year or so. It is a synthetic hormone which, if given daily before an anticipated estrus, prevents the dog from coming into season. As soon as the treatment is stopped, the normal ovarian cycle resumes. This may prove a happy, though possibly expensive, solution for cat owners who do not want to rule out the possibility of kittens permanently but would like to have some control over the spacing of litters. This medication can be had only on prescription from a vet.

If your female has been bred, kittens may be expected in about sixty-one days. The mother doesn't require any special attention, nor should she be confined or kept from normal exercise. She does need a varied, high quality diet, not only for her own health, but for the development of the kittens. And she should be kept free of internal and external parasites. As the pregnancy advances, one usually notices that the cat is less active and agile and that of her own accord she cuts down on jumping and climbing. Her appetite often increases perceptibly in the last three weeks of gestation, and she is apt to spend a good deal of time licking at her abdomen and tail region. Licking, incidentally, is not purely a cleaning device in felines. It appears also to have important stimulating effects in giving birth. Lionesses have been observed, during the final days of pregnancy, thoughtfully plucking out the fur around their nipples with their teeth. I have never seen a domestic cat do this, and with longhairs especially, nursing is easier for the kittens if the fur around the nipples is clipped with a scissors.

Human and feline notions of the perfect nest for kittens are often at wide variance. Countless owners provide what they think will be perfect quarters for the accouchement, only to have their cat choose the coat closet with its floor heaped with galoshes instead. You are apt to have better luck if you keep in mind what the cat considers essential for raising kittens. She wants a spot that is dark and undisturbed, that will be dry and protected from wind and that, preferably, has a soft bottom. A cardboard carton, about a foot and a half square with sides about a foot high, makes a perfectly satisfactory bed. An old bath towel, hay, straw, or shredded newspaper can be used to cover the bottom. Sawdust or fine shavings are not recommended for two reasons. The kittens may snuffle it up their noses, and the soiled sawdust is likely to cling to their coats. If the mother cat seems to find the bed you provide acceptable, be sure that she also agrees to its location. If, after the kittens are born, she doesn't approve, she will transport them one by one to some other nest which may not suit you at all.

Until the kittens are old enough to leave the nest, the mother keeps it as clean as possible by consuming their eliminations, as dogs do, and scientific opinion is that the less one interferes with her sanitary arrangements the better. One research laboratory found that when they handled the kittens and changed the bedding daily, a number of mothers would attack and kill their young. Some even ate the entire litter. Others urinated on the kittens or disowned them, and the kittens died within a few days. As an experiment, the laboratory switched from paper to hay bedding which was left undisturbed for several weeks, and the kittens were not handled unless it was absolutely necessary. Fatalities decreased sharply.

A cat's restlessness, as well as certain physical signs, usually make it obvious when the kittens are about to be born. The mother's breasts may ooze colostrum (the fluid which precedes milk) and her vulva will be distended. She will scratch repeatedly at her bed, wander aimlessly around, lap often from her water bowl and squat from time to time as though she were straining to defecate. Some cats, particularly Siamese, call as though they were in season in these first stages. This behavior may go on for several hours before any contractions start. It may take the cat anywhere from one to twelve hours to produce her litter. If her labor goes beyond that time, it is wise to get medical help. In the womb, each kitten is encased in its own amniotic sac. Sometimes kittens are born with the sac still intact around them; sometimes they are still in the sac although it has ruptured; still others may emerge without the sac, which must follow with the placenta. The normal procedure for the mother is to lick roughly at the sack, releasing the kitten, then chew off the navel cord and consume all of the afterbirth. Between the appearance of each kitten she divides her attention between disposing of the sac, licking the newborn dry and licking at herself, apparently to help stimulate passage of the next kitten. She doesn't necessarily give the newborn priority in these attentions. Opinion is divided as to how much human aid and encouragement the mother wants during the birth of her kittens. My own feeling is that ordinarily she will manage best on her own, though if human stroking or conversation seems to comfort her, it does no harm.

Kittens are, of course, blind as well as quite immature at birth. Their eyes normally open when they are about a week old. Kittens do not start nursing immediately after birth. It may be an hour or so before they blunder into a nipple and settle down to nurse. While she is giving birth to the later kittens, the mother's attention to the first-born may appear to be rather absentminded. She may spend more time licking at herself than licking them and she may ignore for the moment their plaintive squeaks. Within twenty-four hours, though, the mother has usually gamely shouldered all her maternal responsibilities. She licks her children regularly, which not only keeps them clean but stimulates them, she arranges herself in the nest so that she is encircling them, and she quickly retrieves any kitten that may have blindly staggered off to a corner. This behavior is not reasoned, but is the result of hormonal stimulation that accompanies the birth process. Just as the mother is hormonally stimulated to bite off the umbilical cord in such a manner that it is automatically clamped to prevent hemorrhage, so her reactions to her kittens happily, though unpremeditatedly, promote their welfare.

Abnormal maternal behavior is comparatively rare in domestic cats and less well understood. Extreme examples, which have already been mentioned, are killing or rejecting the kittens. More common is the inept mother who steps or lies on her babies, allows them to stray, or to settle down outside the warmth of her encircling body. However, by and large, cats are extremely deft with their young, and no more is required from the owner than a discreet watchfulness to see that a runty kitten isn't being discriminated against by its stronger siblings. Lionesses have been observed to eat their newborn offspring through what appeared to be misplaced zeal; the mother begins to devour the afterbirth and cord while it is still attached to the cub and just keeps on eating when she gets to the cub. In contrast, a domestic cat rarely destroys a kitten at birth. When infanticide occurs, it is usually a few days later, and often after the kittens have been handled a good deal by people. One possible explanation of this is that it is a reaction to danger; the mother feels menaced by human intrusion and destroys the kittens rather than cope with the burden they present in the face of danger. On this assumption it is common practice among professionals to handle newborn kittens, when necessary, with leather gloves so that the human smell will not contaminate them in the mother's nose. Finally, as they do in almost everything, cats vary tremendously in their reactions to motherhood. Socksie, one of the gentlest and most affectionate cats we ever had, was adamant about having her kittens in secrecy. I have known other cats, though, that seemed to be inordinately pleased at my interest in their offspring and if I didn't already know where the nest was, would proudly lead me to it. The key to success as a godparent is to exercise tact and take your cues from the mother cat.

Occasionally it happens that a mother cat dies in birth or while the kittens are still very young. The cat's owner is then faced with three possible courses: one is to humanely do away with the kittens; another is to look for a nursing cat willing to act as foster mother; the third is to raise the kittens by hand. I suggest this as the final alternative because, unless the kittens are show cats of championship stock and the owner is determined to preserve them, it is not the wisest course.

Raising kittens from birth by hand is a tremendous undertaking and the results are often not worth the labor. Very much like baby monkeys that have been experimentally raised in laboratories with dummy mothers, kittens raised by hand often show distinct signs of emotional and social deprivation. They have missed all the instruction in behavior and social relations their mother would have given them and often seem when grown, according to one authority, to be quite unsure of their identity. They are likely to be dirty in their habits and almost impossible to housebreak. They do not, in short, make very desirable pets.

However, if for emotional or financial reasons, one is determined to try being a foster parent, here is what is involved: For the first few days after birth, the kittens will need to be fed at two-hour intervals around the clock. A standard formula is: one-half cup evaporated milk to one-half cup water, one tablespoon of Karo syrup and one strained egg yolk. The amount to be given at each feeding is about a quarter of an ounce, but one should stop at any point before that if the kitten's belly starts looking distended. This formula can be given either in a doll's nursing bottle or a medicine dropper. In either case it requires deftness and alertness to make sure the kitten doesn't: a) snuff the milk up its nose, b) choke, c) fail to get any. After each feeding, the kitten's rear end should be gently rubbed with a piece of cotton soaked in warm mineral oil to make it urinate and defecate, and the results wiped off.

After a few days the time between feedings can be increased to every three or four hours, with the kitten getting slightly more at each feeding. The cleaning process will have to be continued until the kittens are old enough to use a sanitary tray at three or four weeks.

Keeping orphaned kittens sufficiently warm also presents a problem. A not-very-hot hot water bottle wrapped in a towel and placed at the back of their nest is one solution, but not a long-lasting one. The water will have to be changed every few hours. An electric heating pad can also be used for the first week or so, but not after the kittens' milk teeth come in.

When the kittens are three or four weeks old, steady on their feet, with their eyes open, their milk teeth starting and their stomachs ready for meat, the human foster parent is over the hump, and usually ready for a long rest.

A feline foster mother that has lost her own kittens or has enough milk for extra ones is likely to raise orphans more successfully than a human can, since if she accepts the kittens she will take care of all their needs and oversee their social development. A foster mother usually is not fussy about accepting strange babies provided they are roughly the same age as her own. To ensure a friendly introduction, rub the foster mother thoroughly with a soft cloth, then rub the orphans with the same cloth so they will smell familiar to the mother. If, as occasionally happens, she shows any signs of rejecting the kittens, it is not wise to leave them with her since she may kill them. When kittens lose their own mother at birth, they also lose much of the natural immunity to disease which she would have transmitted to them in the colostrum milk. This means they are considerably more susceptible to stray germs and should be guarded more carefully from infection.

If kittens are unwanted or cannot be properly cared for, the only decent thing to do is to destroy them at birth or within a day or so thereafter. It is much crueler to let them grow up and then abandon them or to postpone their demise until they are mature enough to be conscious of what is happening to them. When I was a child, the gardener usually disposed of unwanted kittens by drowning them in a pail. I still recall with a shudder watching this gruesome operation. The kittens, even newborn ones, struggled and floundered and seemed to take forever to die. It is a method absolutely without merit. A far simpler and more humane way to dispose of a litter of newborn kittens is to put them in a fairly small box with a wad of cotton soaked in ether or chloroform. In a matter of minutes they will have been painlessly put to sleep. If the whole idea of disposing of kittens yourself seems too ghastly—and there is nothing sissyish in this reaction—waste no time in taking them to a local humane association or to a veterinarian.

Drying up the milk of a mother who has lost her kittens is no problem at all. Just leave her alone, and in a few days her milk will taper off to nothing. Rubbing the nipples with camphorated oil is not recommended; it simply stimulates the manufacture of more milk. There is no special advantage, either, in leaving the mother one kitten. As long as she has a kitten to nurse she will continue to have milk, and a lone kitten has rather a thin time of it.

Determining the sex of kittens, or even of full grown cats, seems to present great difficulties for many people. It is confusing because toms have nipples as females do, the penis is sheathed inside the body and the testicles, under their fur, hug the body tightly. However, an observant eye will be able to detect that in one instance the opening below the rectum is in the shape of a circle, while in the other it is in the shape of a slit. The circle, which belongs to a tom, is placed farther from the rectum than is the slit. Making the distinction is easier if you have opposites to compare. However, if you are still unable to determine visually by the time the kittens are three months old, a gentle exploration between openings usually reveals the testicles.

Chapter V

The Well-Groomed Cat

Except in extraordinary circumstances, cats do not need baths. A healthy cat never has a bad smell. The cat is equipped with sweat glands, as well as the sebaceous glands that discharge minute amounts of a waxy substance called sebum into the hair follicles to help make its coat waterproof and shiny, but these secretions do not give the coat any unpleasant smell. Normally, the skin itself is kept clean by a constant process of shedding and self-renewal. Consequently, all that routine washing with soap or a detergent shampoo accomplishes is to remove the essential oils from the cat's coat, leaving the skin more vulnerable to attack by disease organisms. There is, too, the possibility that the cat's resistance to respiratory infection may be lowered; a Rockefeller Foundation study showed that feline pneumonitis, for instance, could be induced by stress. The injury to the cat's psyche alone has not, so far as I know, yet been studied.

The Well-Groomed Cat

In most cases, dampening with clear water and rubbing vigorously with a towel will remove any dirt a cat has picked up, but there are occasions when a thorough shampooing is the only possible solution. Minnie's acquisition was such an occasion. When I first met Minnie as a kitten disconsolately sniffing a small mound of garbage in a New York gutter, she was so extraordinarily filthy that it was quite impossible to tell what proportion of her was dirt and what cat. If we were to live together, as we impetuously decided to do, she obviously had to have a bath. I must admit that when I saw her wet—undressed, so to speak—I had grave second thoughts. Fortunately this impression lasted no longer than her bath.

There are various locations in which to give a bath, the aim being to make it is swift, efficient and painless as possible. The cat's distaste for the project is based more on fear and dislike of restraint, of the slippery footing and of the unexpectedness of its situation than on a fear of water. Many cats, both wild and domestic, enjoy swimming and fishing. In fact, an acquaintance of mine is the hapless owner of a tom named Zooey who is mad about swimming in the bathtub. If Zooey's owner wants to take a bath without him, she has to lock the door before running the tub, then wash to the accompaniment of a concert of scratching and reproaching outside the bathroom. I have always used the bathtub, rather than a washtub on a table, for bathing pets, because the ease of rinsing seems to me to outweigh the inconvenience of having to squat beside it. Besides, the slippery bottom with its lack of toe-hold is a great help in keeping ten pounds of soaking outrage from scrambling out of one's grasp. It is safer, neater and kinder not to draw any water in the tub, but simply to use a hand spray or pitcher to wet the cat down before soaping and to rinse it afterward. Liquid soaps lather more quickly than cake soaps; a good one is Johnson's baby shampoo. It is mild and formulated not to sting if one inadvertently gets some in the cat's eyes. My mother, who taught me how to bathe animals, always began lathering with a ring of suds around the neck on the theory that this kept the fleas at one end from migrating to the other. Actually, it makes little difference, since they drown anyway. However, while we're on the subject of fleas, a bath, with or without vermicidal soap, is not an efficient way to get rid of them. Though it drowns whatever fleas are on the cat at the moment, it has no effect in repelling new boarders lurking around the house. To finish off a bath, the cat should be thoroughly dried, then thoroughly brushed and, to be on the safe side, kept indoors for several hours.

While bathing a cat is usually a once-in-a-lifetime affair, brushing and combing are routine necessities. The purpose, of course, is to get rid of dead hair, dead skin particles, and dust. If this is not done by combing, the cat will endeavor to do it by licking. The most serious result may be hairballs (an accumulation of hair in the cat's stomach, discussed in Chapter VII) while the merely annoying one is the accumulation of hair on furniture and clothes—and a less glossy coat on the cat. One might quibble that no one regularly brushes cats in the wild, yet their coats seem healthy and glossy. As a matter of fact, a cat that spends much time out-of-doors does get groomed regularly. It is brushed constantly by tall grasses, twigs and underbrush as it goes about its daily business. That is why a short-haired country cat needs least grooming by its owner, while a city cat, especially a longhaired variety, needs most.

To keep a long-haired cat's coat in top condition, it should be groomed daily. Brushing alone is not enough, since it won't remove hair mats. The approved technique is to comb first with a single-row steel comb—it pays to invest in the best you can find—to get snarls out before they turn into mats, then to brush, which stimulates the skin and distributes the oils, leaving the cat's coat with a high gloss. In the case of long-hairs, an ounce of prevention is worth more than a pound of cure. It takes only a moment to go through the cat's coat with a comb every day, whereas, if you wait until it has matted, it can take hours and hours, with much resultant bad feeling, to pull or cut the mats out. It is always a good idea to get a cat used to the idea of brushing and combing while it's young and impressionable; this is especially true with long-haired cats for which combing is so vital. It can take as many as three strong people, or anesthesia, to accomplish the grooming of a full-grown long-hair that resists these attentions.

Even the most fastidious cat occasionally blunders into wet paint. Aside from the damage to its looks, there is the danger that there may be toxic pigments in the paint which will poison the cat when it tries to lick them off. Both paint and tar should be removed at once, but not with turpentine, which will burn the skin. The remedy is to rub a vegetable oil into the coat in sufficient quantity to make an emulsion with the paint and dissolve it, then wash both off with a detergent. Once paint has dried on a cat's coat, there's nothing to do but cut out as much as possible and wait for the hair to grow.

Cats seems far cleverer than dogs about keeping out of the way of skunks, but once in a while even they fail to dodge in time. When this happens, the treatment is to rinse the cat as soon as possible with a mildly acid solution such as tomato juice or an ounce of vinegar in a pint of warm water to neutralize the skunk's spray, which is alkaline. It may have to be repeated several times, with a water rinse in between. If the results seem discouraging while the coat is wet, remember that it will smell much less as soon as it dries.

Claws usually present a problem only in the case of the

indoor cat which has no place to wear them down except on your favorite upholstered chair. Sometimes a scratching post solves this problem (see Chapter II). If the cat, nevertheless, continues to shred the furniture or wallpaper, you will have to cast about for another solution. One is to have the front claws surgically removed. I have no experience with this myself and rather shrink from the idea, but my vet swears that it causes neither pain nor psychic trauma, that the cat doesn't seem to miss the claws in the least, that, in fact, its front pads become callused so that they are just as useful for climbing and digging, and much less damaging. A cat's hind claws should never be tampered with; without them it can't climb to safety if confronted with danger, and, in any case, it isn't the hind claws that do the damage. Some owners of apartment-pent cats solve the scratching problem by trimming the front claws regularly. There's little danger of hurting the cat or damaging its claws if you are careful to trim off only the transparent part of the claw and not cut below the quick. Patent claw clippers are sold in pet shops for this purpose; the vest-pocket nail clippers are also good. Scissors, on the other hand, are not recommended, because they squeeze the nail. How easy this operation is depends on how docile the cat is—none likes restraint—and, to end on a discouraging note, it must be mentioned that clipping is something of a losing battle—it has to be repeated every five to seven days.

Though healthy cats have no perceptible body odor, some, unfortunately, do have bad breath. If a cat's coat does have a bad smell, there is a good chance that the smell originated in the mouth and was deposited on the cat's coat by licking. There are a number of possible causes for bad breath. In most cases a vet can diagnose and treat them, and it is important that he should. Even if they are not signals that something serious is wrong, it is distressing both for you and the cat if you have to turn your head every time it approaches you.

Cats fed on an exclusively soft diet are apt to have unhealthy gums and tartar on their teeth, and this is the most common cause of bad breath. It is a good idea to take a look at the cat's teeth regularly. If there is much tartar, it should be scraped off, perhaps as often as every six months. Some intrepid owners undertake the job themselves. The first step is to pop puss into a restraining sack, and the whole thing may be a pretty flummoxing affair for both parties. I would rather leave it to the vet.

Sometimes cats develop diseases like gingivitis, or trench mouth, as a result of vitamin deficiencies, and these cause bad breath. Felines are as unwise as infants about the objects they put in their mouths, and it is not unusual for threaded needles, sharp sticks or bone splinters to become lodged in the gums. After making an initial fuss, the cat seems to forget they are there, and the foreign body often creates an infection that gives rise to an unmistakably foul smell. More unusual causes of bad breath are tumors of the mouth membrane.

Possibly the most elusive cause of chronic halitosis is acid stomach. We now know that some highly nervous cats, like some nervous people, burp up stomach acids, making their breath smell very bad indeed. Unhappily, this is a permanent condition, and the best you can do is to try to modify the acidity by adding a pinch of bicarbonate of soda to the cat's milk, by mixing cottage cheese in with its food, by feeding small meals frequently—or all three.

The feline ear is a splendid organ, one of the most sensitive instruments of hearing in the animal world. Unfortunately, an unpleasant little parasite, *Otodectes cynotis*, commonly called the ear mite, finds the ear of the cat splendid as a habitat. The mites do not burrow under the skin but usually congregate deep in the ear canal near the drum, sucking blood through the delicate skin there. The resulting congestion and irritation of the ear canal is called ear mange and is quite common. My vet tells me that at least fifty per cent of the cats he sees in his practice suffer from it. Because clearing up ear mange may be a long tedious business, it is wise to inspect closely the ears of any cat you are thinking of acquiring before you make up your mind. If they are not perfectly clean, with a glistening, healthy-looking surface, choose another cat.

Often a cat with ear mites lets you know about it by shaking its head or clawing frantically at its ears. It may even run around in circles. However, the cat's behavior is not really a good index to the severity of the infestation. Kittens sometimes are infested from birth and accept the condition with utter resignation; some cats make a tremendous to-do about mites, others seem not to be bothered by them. For this reason, the cat's ears should be checked at regular intervals. Although the mites themselves are large enough to be discernible through a magnifying glass, they are usually so deep inside the ear that a more readily visible sign of their presence is an accumulation in the ear of a crumbly wax—grayish, brown, or black. If you see that, have the vet confirm your diagnosis and outline treatment. It is almost impossible to kill every last mite and egg at one swoop; it may take as long as two months or more of weekly treatments to catch up with all the strays and prevent them from founding a new dynasty of mites.

Aside from mites, cats have very few ear troubles. They do not require routine cleaning, and poking around in them is more likely to result in injury than any benefit. The term ear canker, one of those vague labels like grippe, is used to cover a variety of unhealthy conditions of the ear, usually secondary infections that the cat's clawing for ear mites has created. The symptoms may be an accumulation of wax, a bad smell in the ears, continued scratching, or all three. They warrant a trip to the vet. Since this is such a sensitive area, continued irritation can make a cat thin, rundown and nervous, while continued clawing at the ears can disfigure them as well as set up secondary infections.

Fleas still hold the title of being the commonest and most troublesome of the external parasites to which cats are hosts. Among their more unpleasant characteristics is their ability to spread tapeworm and heartworm in the animal world. Possibly they spread other skin diseases of cats, as well. At the very least, they annoy their feline hosts continually, spoil the looks of their coats, and, if they are sufficiently hungry, have no qualms about biting people. There are numerous types of fleas, but all share the same sort of life cycle, which is the important thing to know in trying to get rid of them.

All fleas go through four life stages—egg, larva, pupa and adult—and choose different locations for the different stages, which is why they are so hard to eradicate. The female lays her eggs on the host but the eggs, instead of staying there, drop off and may land in crevices of furniture, cracks in the floor, in the pile of rugs and so forth. The eggs develop into larvae, which feed on dust, flakes of dead skin from the host and similar matter. In about two weeks the larvae are full grown and spin tiny cocoons in which they are transformed into pupae. Roughly a week later, the pupa changes into an adult flea, out for blood. It is therefore of utmost importance to de-flea the premises as well as the cat.

Until recently, de-fleaing the cat was not an easy matter. Many of the insecticides and flea powders that can be used for dogs are unsafe for cats because cats are such indefatigable lickers. The commonly recommended remedy was a flea powder based on rotenone and derris root. This was not poisonous to the cat if swallowed, but it was not terribly discouraging to the flea, either. Now, however, there are several new, safe and potent chemicals which make the treatment simple and effective. A veterinarian can tell you the newest and best. To get rid of flea larvae and pupae which may be lurking around the premises, spray the floors and lower portions of the walls with a commercial insecticide at regular intervals. There are several, most often based on pyrethrums, that are safe both for people and cats; the labels usually specify this. But in any case, it is a wise precaution to keep the cat out of the room until the spray has settled. And, in keeping the house flea-free, do not overlook the cat's bedding. It should be washed frequently.

Lice, happily, are rather rare in the United States these days, though occasionally they are a problem in rural areas. Also they are considerably easier to get rid of than fleas because they spend their entire life cycle on the host. The most obvious sign of their presence is usually the thousands of tiny eggs or nits glued to individual hairs on a cat's coat. Anything that kills fleas will also kill lice.

Though lice seem to be on the wane, ticks seem to be on the wax. Some summers they are enough to drive a country-living dog owner mad. They do not appear to infest cats—that is, literally cover them from head to foot—as they do dogs, but they occasionally fasten on to some part of the cat's body that it cannot reach with its teeth, like head and ears, and even an occasional tick is one too many. Like fleas, they spend portions of their lives off the host—meaning in cracks of woodwork, under carpets, behind pictures or wall ornaments—and, like fleas, some varieties are disease carriers. If you are not faced with removing vast numbers of ticks from your pet, and you're not likely to be with a cat, the approved method is to remove and destroy them one by one. On the host, the tick's manner of operation is to fasten its fangs into the animal's hide and sink in its sharp proboscis to suck blood. Yanking ticks off with the fingers is not recommended for two reasons: the fangs and proboscis are very likely to remain embedded in the host where their presence creates a chemical reaction which can cause sore, itchy lumps or abscesses. It is also wiser not to touch ticks on the possibility that they may be a disease-bearing variety. To make sure of removing the tick in toto you may use a drop of ether, which will relax it, or a drop of mineral oil which will suffocate it. After half an hour or so, a pair of tweezers easily removes the inert body. There are also new tick preparations available these days. Sprayed on a small wad of cotton and held over the tick, they give the *coup de grâce* with ease and speed. If you remove a relaxed, but live, tick, dispatch it immediately, either by burning it with a match (it pops like popcorn—a rather grisly form of entertainment when I was a child) or by dropping it into a can of kerosene. It is very hard to squash a tick.

There are many popular books about the care of cats which give the impression that one needs to be a practicing dermatologist to live with a cat. There is no doubt that skin ailments may be maddeningly elusive to diagnose and frustratingly slow to clear up, leaving a dramatic memory of a siege with them in the owner's mind. It is also true that there are a number of skin troubles a cat can have, but the chances of any one cat's having any or many of them are small. Cats are, for instance, much less prone to skin trouble than dogs. Nevertheless, forewarned is forearmed, and if you know what the symptoms of skin diseases look like, you are less apt to unwittingly acquire a pet already infected with one of them.

Ringworm, which is caused by a fungus similar to that which causes athlete's foot, belongs in that unpleasant category called zoonoses—meaning it can be, and frequently is, swapped back and forth between humans and animals. Cats seem to be much more susceptible in this case than are dogs, and ringworm can be highly infectious. Unfortunately, it is far easier to spot ringworm on human skin than on a cat, so often the cat isn't suspected until every member of the family is scratching wildly. Although its common name implies a symmetrical ring—and that is what people usually look for —ringworm patches are more often roughly oval in shape, or may even masquerade as some other skin trouble that causes bald patches. They have a tendency to appear most often around a cat's head and neck, though they may turn up anywhere. Untreated, a ringworm lesion may eventually cure itself, but another turns up somewhere else. Until recently, ringworm was rather discouraging to treat because of this characteristic, but nowadays there is an internal remedy that gives dramatic results in preventing reproduction of the spores. This is not a fungicide, though; the lesions already on the skin still have to be treated independently. A cat with ringworm should be taken to the vet as soon as any symptoms are spotted.

Mange breaks down, as far as cats are concerned, into two varieties. One is cat mange caused by a mite named *Notoedres Cati*, a close relative of the mite that much more frequently causes sarcoptic mange in dogs. The other, and more severe, variety is variously known as follicular, demodectic, or red mange. It is very rare in cats. Only a veterinarian can diagnose mange positively, and any symptoms such as bald spots, scurfy or reddened patches of skin, or frantic scratching are grounds for hustling a cat right off for a consultation. Young cats, for some reason, seem to be far more susceptible to mange than older ones. But the disease—either variety—is nothing to fool with at any age.

There are certain sanitary precautions that should be taken in the event of skin disease symptoms, not only to speed the cat's recovery, but to guard against spreading the disease. Isolation, in a cage if possible, is the ideal. In any case, the cat should be confined to one room, and disposable bedding, such as newspaper which can be burned daily, should be used. Nothing short of physical restraint can persuade a cat not to bite and lick at skin lesions. Two handy preventive devices are the Elizabethan collar and the head funnel. The collar looks like what its name implies—a wide ruff of heavy cardboard. To make one, cut out a doughnut with a hole large enough to go around the cat's neck, then cut it in half and punch holes along the cuts so that it may be laced together when it is in place. A head funnel can be improvised from something as simple as an ice cream container or round plastic refrigerator container with the bottom taken out and holes punched along the bottom edge so that it can be tied to a collar. Wearing either of these devices, the cat can see and eat perfectly well, but can't bite at sores or claw at its head with much success.

Dandruff is an annoying, though rarely serious problem for cats. Though the specific causes of it are not known, it appears to have a good deal to do with the circulation of the blood vessels under the skin and the amount of debris on the skin. Cats that spend their lives in steam-heated apartments and poorly fed cats are the usual sufferers. Often, more frequent brushing takes care of the problem. If it doesn't, a veterinarian can prescribe one of the selinium products which seem to work very well. Caution, though; these are toxic and must be used with care.

The causes of eczema are as mysterious in cats as they are

in human beings. Researchers now think that in many cases eczema is caused by an allergy. To make matters more confusing, there are often popular references to wet and dry eczema, as though these were distinct varieties. Actually, wet and dry refer only to the appearance of the skin. If the cat bites and licks a great deal at an eczematous patch, it will indeed look wet, and secondary infections may develop to complicate the picture even further. In any case, it takes tremendous patience and diligence on the part of the cat's owner, backed up by a treatment plan from a veterinarian, to clear up a case of eczema.

Chapter VI

First Aid for the Injured

The most accident-prone age in the human span is between one and three, the toddling stage, when babies suddenly become mobile enough to explore their surroundings but haven't the experience to recognize the potential dangers. This is the plight of cats all their lives, as they meet the hazards domestication involves. Almost any jam a baby can get itself into, a cat can too, plus a few others, like falling from high places or getting its tail slammed in a door. With luck, the resulting injury may be trifling; frequently, though, prompt and skillful emergency treatment can mean the difference between complete recovery and permanent maiming, or even between life and death.

For several reasons, first aid is a tricky subject to advise on at long distance. The wrong treatment or clumsy treatment can, in some instances, be worse than none at all. And, if one is adept at home doctoring there is the temptation to try to treat injuries that really require a veterinarian's skill and knowledge. But if one keeps firmly in mind that first aid should be no more than its name implies—what to do until the doctor comes—knowing how to handle certain emergencies and how to use some simple nursing techniques is invaluable to any cat owner.

When cats are frightened or in pain they are notably unreasonable. Any tendencies toward gratitude or cooperativeness that they might harbor in ordinary circumstances are replaced by impulses to fight or to escape the human hand that's trying to help them. Thus, the first step to take with an injured cat is to figure out a way to keep it still long enough to examine or treat it without getting clawed or bitten in the process. How you do this may vary with the circumstances and the injury, but any approach will be more successful if you can give the cat a few minutes to calm down and if you treat it calmly yourself.

Usually the most successful way to pick up a resisting cat is by the scruff of the neck, provided, of course, the cat's injury isn't in the head or neck region. This grip does not hurt a cat, but it does have a subduing effect. Just the same, it is a wise precaution to wear leather gloves whenever you are dealing with a cat that's upset.

A grip on the cat's neck can't be maintained indefinitely; it simply gives you time to decide what to do next. And the next step depends on whether you are handling the animal alone or have someone to help you, where the cat's injury is, and just how wild it is at the moment. It may take two people to hold a cat still long enough for any thorough examination or bandaging. Failing an assistant, a restraining sack can be used. Heavy canvas bags with zippers are sold in pet shops for this purpose, but in an emergency a sturdy laundry bag with a drawstring neck or even a bath towel or small rug wrapped around the cat will do. Trying to tie a cat's mouth shut is not advised; it is extremely difficult to do without getting clawed. The disadvantage of a restraining sack is that while it keeps the cat from scratching or escaping, it may also conceal the part of the cat that is injured. The only way out of this difficulty is to put only half the cat into the sack— the end you don't want to examine. Quite possibly such extreme measures won't be necessary. Often standing the cat on a slippery surface such as a kitchen table and holding it in the crook of your arm with a firm grip on the nape of its neck will keep it sufficiently immobilized to be looked over. However, with no assistant, no sack, no kitchen table, and a really hysterical cat, it is best to give up the idea of treating it at home, and roll it firmly in a heavy towel or blanket or put it into a container and speed it to the veterinarian.

Once you have mastered the basic skill of handling a sick or injured cat you will find that the things you are most frequently required to do are to take temperature and give medicine, both in pill and liquid form. Unless a cat is remarkably calm and cooperative—or weak—two people are needed to take its temperature. It is easiest to do if you stand the cat on a slippery surface and have an assistant hold the cat's head and front feet. An ordinary rectal thermometer, liberally greased with vasoline, is the standard equipment. It should remain in place two to three minutes, if you can manage it.

The normal body temperature for a cat is approximately 101 degrees, but fright or excitement can shoot it up a degree or more above that. This is why veterinarians ask an owner to take a sick cat's temperature at home. If it can be done without flustering the cat too badly, the reading is apt to be more accurate than it will be after a ride to the vet's office and the added nervousness his examining room induces.

It takes practice to become deft at dosing cats; they are even more uncooperative than dogs about taking medicine. Until you become adept, it's best to have someone help you hold your patient; once your hand becomes practiced, it's often possible to administer medicine so swiftly that before the cat knows it, it's swallowed. Usually the only hazard in giving pills is that the cat will promptly spit them out. Liquid medicine, on the other hand, presents the more serious danger of getting into the cat's lungs. That is why it is not recommended to squirt in a large amount and clamp the cat's jaws shut on it; the cat is apt to cough or choke and drive some of the medicine into its lungs. One possible result of this is pneumonia. The most successful technique is to sit the cat on a table and have an assistant hold its front paws with one hand, while with the other he tilts the cat's head up until its nose points at the ceiling. You then slide a finger between its lips and pull out the skin at the corner of the mouth to make a pocket; into this you pour the medicine a bit at a time. As it runs over the back of the tongue, the cat usually swallows—if the medicine isn't too unpalatable. Sweet, syrupy medicine, incidentally, is very hard to get down cats; it makes them drool.

The technique for pill giving is simpler. Again the cat's nose should be pointing toward the ceiling. With the fingers of one hand you gently force its jaws open; with the other you quickly drop the pill as far back on its tongue as you can. Usually, it will go right down, but to make sure hold a pencil in the same hand as the pill and, as soon as the pill is in, give it a poke with the eraser end. Once a pill is down, it rarely comes back. Some owners who find themselves unequal to this task resort to subterfuge to get medicine into their pets, concealing it in the middle of a tasty ball of food. If the medicine is really unpleasant, it will be hard to fool a cat more than once with this trick.

Once familiar with the basic skills of nursing a sick pet, you will be better able to deal with the more common emergencies a cat owner is most likely to face. They are listed below in the order of their frequency, with brief recommendations as to what to do or not do about them.

BITES from other cats, from dogs and from rats are the number-one injury to cats. Bites make puncture wounds which are nasty things to deal with because of the germs deposited by the biter's teeth and because the surface skin is likely to close over them and create a perfect pocket in which infection and abscesses can develop. Prompt and thorough cleaning of the wound is the first-aid requisite here. Wash it gently with a mild soap and water on a piece of cotton, rinse it well and finish by dropping in an antiseptic with a medicine dropper. The safest antiseptic to use with cats is peroxide. None of the phenol derivatives, such as lysol, should ever be used; they are highly toxic to cats. If no swelling develops and the wound appears to be healing from the bottom up, professional treatment usually is not necessary. But if there is pronounced swelling around the wound, it may mean an abscess is forming, and this should be treated without delay by a veterinarian.

If you happen to be on the scene, the safest way to break up a fight is to use the old method of throwing cold water on the combatants. Don't, in any circumstances, wade into the fray; you are likely to be bitten by both parties. If there's no water handy, use anything that will distract the animals without involving you physically.

AUTOMOBILE ACCIDENTS befall cats with distressing regularity in the suburbs and the country. If the cat isn't killed outright, it is very likely to suffer internal injuries or broken bones. Fractures are not always easy to spot. Shock, paleness of the tongue and lips may indicate internal injuries. In either case, do not attempt any treatment yourself. Get the cat to the vet or, preferably, the vet to the cat as quickly as you can, meanwhile moving the cat as little as possible. Sometimes a lucky cat is hit by a car and gets off with nothing worse than bruises or abrasions, which means that patches of hair have been scraped off and the skin left raw or bleeding. This sort of injury usually needs no more than gentle washing with soap and water and application of an antiseptic. Ordinarily, bandaging is unnecessary and, unless signs of infection develop, treatment by a vet is not called for.

CUTS from sharp objects such as broken glass, barbed wire, tin cans and so on are almost inevitable in the life of a normally adventuresome cat. These cuts are most often in the pads or lower legs where they cause profuse bleeding. The immediate problem with cuts of this variety is to stop the bleeding. To do this, you use a pressure bandage, which means pressing a piece of wadded cloth or gauze against the wound, then wrapping a bandage tightly around it. Don't be afraid to wrap it tightly, provided you make certain that the pressure extends evenly to the end of the extremity. If an artery has been cut, and blood is gushing so freely that a pressure bandage won't control it, a tourniquet can be used for wounds on the legs or tail. A tourniquet for a cat is tied just like a tourniquet for a human, at any point between the wound and the animal's body. We used to be told that a tourniquet should be loosened every ten minutes. Nowadays, veterinarians believe it is better not to loosen it, but leave it in place until you can get the cat to an animal hospital, for the chances are that any cat bleeding profusely enough to need a pressure bandage or a tourniquet, also needs to see a doctor.

FOREIGN BODIES in mouth, stomach, or in the rectum come next on the list of hazards, for cats are notoriously unwise about putting odd objects in their mouths. Removing foreign bodies usually is most skillfully and painlessly done in the veterinarian's office. The cat owner's main responsibility here is in noticing that something is wrong. If a cat claws at its mouth or refuses to eat, in spite of seeming hungry, it is likely to have a small stick, a sliver of bone or a threaded needle wedged in its mouth. Sometimes these can be removed at home; it is always worth taking a look in any case. However, if you are going to undertake to remove it yourself, put on gloves first.

An owner might suspect a foreign body in the stomach if a cat seems nauseated, retches or vomits with no fever or other sign of illness, and has scanty stools or no stool. String and hairballs (see Chapter VII) are the commonest offenders in this case. Often one or two teaspoonfuls of mineral oil will pass the object along. If it doesn't, consult a vet.

An alert owner who notices a cat straining or crying when it defecates, and possibly even passing a little blood, has cause to believe there is a foreign body in the cat's rectum. Again removal is best undertaken by a vet.

Nine times out of ten when a cat swallows something it shouldn't, human carelessness is more to blame than the cat. Threaded needles left lying around, pieces of string or balls of yarn given to the cat as toys, are invitations to trouble.

BEING BURNED OR SCALDED usually doesn't happen to a cat

more than once in its lifetime, for cats learn fast to keep away from hot things. But before the lesson has been absorbed you may have to treat a pet that has burned its pads by jumping onto a hot stove or radiator or scalded itself by overturning a saucepan of boiling liquid. The preferred first aid for burns and scalds is to apply ice packs or run cold water over the area immediately and keep it up until you can get medical care. Since it's well nigh impossible to hold a squirming cat under a faucet for more than a minute, an ice pack or even a freezer bag filled with ice cubes is more practical. Any but the most minor burns should have medical attention, since home treatment is almost impossible. Ordinary burn ointments are useless; the cat will lick them right off and they may be toxic. And unless a serious burn is properly bandaged, the cat's licking is apt to promote secondary infections.

POISONING is probably the most difficult of all emergencies to deal with. It is vital to act fast, keep calm and discover what poison is involved—none of which is easy in the circumstances. In the first place, unless you actually see the cat eating a poisonous substance, you cannot be sure what is wrong, because the symptoms of poisoning—trembling, pain, vomiting, diarrhea and possibly convulsions—are also symptoms of a number of other ailments. And the treatment for poisoning can be absolutely fatal to a cat suffering from feline distemper, for instance. However, if you are certain the cat has been poisoned, induce vomiting with all possible speed. To do this, make a strong solution of salt and water and force the cat to swallow several tablespoons of it. Then find the poison container and rush it and the cat to the nearest animal hospital or poison control center. If you don't bring the container with you, valuable time may be lost determining what the poison was and what antidote should be used.

Poisoning is the most dramatic instance of an ounce of prevention being worth a pound of cure. Cats most frequently are poisoned by eating poisoned rodents, chewing the leaves of plants that have been sprayed, by being treated with a flea powder based on DDT or other chemicals toxic to them, or by being allowed to come in contact with certain household insecticides. Anyone whose household includes a cat should avoid using these chemicals.

ELECTRIC SHOCKS are what a great many curious kittens get for chewing playfully on electric cords. A shocked cat suddenly stiffens, may urinate involuntarily, may, if the shock is severe, become unconscious or die. Pull out the plug before you go to the cat's aid; otherwise you may get a shock yourself. If the cat is unconscious, mouth-to-mouth breathing is the quickest and most effective way to revive it. The technique for this consists of putting the cat on a table in a prone position, with its forelegs stretched out. Hold its head up with one hand; cup the other over its chest, and place your mouth over the cat's mouth and nose. Breathe out, remove your mouth from the cat's face, then gently press on the cat's chest, as you inhale. Keep up the rhythmic pattern of exhaling and pressing until the cat begins to breathe by itself. One reason this method is more successful than other methods of artificial respiration is that more air actually gets into the lungs; another is that the carbon dioxide you exhale into the cat acts as a stimulant to the breathing center. However, anyone who feels squeamish about mouth-to-mouth breathing can use artificial respiration as a second-best. This is done by laying the cat on its side and placing one hand on its rib cage just behind the forelegs. With fingers outspread, apply pressure to the ribs with the same rhythmical movement that is used in human artificial respiration. Press down and quickly lift up at about two-second intervals. As soon as breathing resumes, call a vet to give the cat further treatment.

The secondary result of an electric shock is often a burned

mouth. Usually it's impossible to medicate this sort of burn and it heals by itself uneventfully, even though it looks frightful at first.

DROWNING is a rare but occasional accident that befalls cats. The treatment is the same as for electric shock. First pick up the cat by its hind legs and swing it rapidly back and forth a few times to drain the water out of its lungs. Then start mouth-to-mouth breathing or other artificial respiration. Pneumonia may be a secondary result of drowning, so a vet should be consulted as soon as the emergency has passed.

BEES, WASPS AND HORNETS don't care in the least whom they sting; the aesthetic cat delicately sniffing a flower is as good a candidate as any. Stings are painful and multiple stings can be serious. If a cat drags home with its mouth open or drooling, its head or mouth suddenly swollen, and in obvious pain, it has possibly had an encounter with one or more stinging insects. An antihistamine is the best first-aid treatment. Almost every household medicine cabinet holds some brand of cold remedy containing an antihistamine and a child's dose of this will do very well in a pinch. If a cat is in great pain or in shock, hurry it to an animal hospital. Superficially, a sting looks like an abscess from a bite. It is easy to distinguish between the two, however, because a sting will usually subside in about twelve hours and an abscess will not.

There are several other conditions in which a cat owner someday or other is likely to find a cat; though they do not, strictly speaking, come under the heading of accidents, they do call for emergency treatment.

SHOCK is one of these. A fall, a hard blow, intense pain, hemorrhaging, massive infection or even fright may produce shock which is, in effect, a state of collapse. The symptoms may vary but usually include shallow breathing, a weak heartbeat that is abnormally fast or slow, apathy or its opposite, nervous anxiety, pale tongue and lips, and prostration. Severe shock, if it is not treated, can be fatal. The first aid treatment for shock is simply to keep the animal warm by covering it. This is not to be confused with actually applying artificial heat to an animal in shock; doing that may make things worse. If the cat is able to drink, give it warm fluids, like consommé, by spoon. Don't force fluids down its throat if it is unconscious. It may take an hour or more for the cat to recover, and it is wisest in any case of shock, whether mild or severe, to consult a vet.

FITS or convulsions are a symptom, not a disease. They can be caused by a wide range of ailments from intestinal parasites to nutritional deficiency, and it takes a professional to diagnose and treat the cause. What laymen need to know is how to handle fits until they subside, for there is no method of stopping them. And the way to do that is simple: leave the animal strictly alone. If it can be guided into a secluded place, fine; if not, leave it where it is and call the doctor. Trying to handle a cat having a fit is asking to be clawed, and does the cat no good at all. Frightening as a convulsion looks, animals rarely injure themselves in the course of one. One convulsion is unlikely to last longer than half an hour, though a cat may have repeated fits over a period of days. The cause invariably should be investigated.

RABIES, although a disease (which will be discussed more fully in the following chapter), deserves mention here because of the vital importance of recognizing its symptoms and acting promptly. Rabies is not as widespread among cats as it is among dogs, but since, unfortunately, most states do not make rabies inoculations compulsory for felines, it does occur. The first symptoms of rabies may develop rather slowly over a period of several days. The most characteristic are: hoarse voice, eccentric appetite, a desire to hide in dark places, and viciousness. If a cat shows any changes in personality or behavior that give you even the slightest reason to suspect rabies, shut it up immediately, using whatever safeguards you can against getting bitten in the process, and report your suspicion to your veterinarian or, lacking one, to the local health officer. Rabies is a hideous disease than can be transmitted to humans by the bite of a rabid animal.

HEAT STROKE isn't usual in cats, but it can happen. A long trip in hot weather in a small, inadequately-ventilated container is the commonest cause. What happens in heat stroke is that the heat-regulating mechanism gets out of whack and the body temperature suddenly soars. Hard breathing, possibly vomiting, and collapse are the symptoms. Heat stroke calls for prompt treatment, consisting of immersing the cat in cold water or wetting it down repeatedly until body temperature is normal. If fast measures aren't taken, heat stroke can result in death.

Chapter VII

Sick as a Cat

Anyone who does much reading about cats is apt to be left with the feeling that, medically speaking, felines are a most contradictory species. That they have endured unchanged for so many thousands of years must mean they are remarkably hardy. The innumerable legends about the ordeals of starvation, confinement, or travel survived by cats bear this out. On the other hand, much of the current literature lists such a vast number of ailments and diseases which can afflict cats that one remembers with difficulty that thousands and thousands of them live happily and uneventfully to old age.

The explanation of this apparent contradiction lies in the very recent development of feline medicine. Fifteen years ago veterinary colleges gave no courses in it; there were no textbooks on the subject. A vet called to treat a sick cat had to rely on his own experience or guesswork, or hope that whatever worked on dogs, rabbits, mink or any of the other small mammals also worked on cats. The picture today is considerably changed. Feline physiology and medicine are being studied intensively and on an ever-widening scale. New drugs and treatments are saving cats that would have died ten years ago. Scientific interest has developed to such a degree that nowadays veterinarians who formerly would have had a small-animal practice may limit their practice exclusively to cats. All this is good news for cats and cat owners. It would be unfortunate, however, if this new emphasis on feline medicine gave anyone the mistaken impression that his cat is necessarily going to contract all or even a few of the diseases that have been recognized so recently.

This chapter, therefore, is deliberately confined to the common internal ailments and the few serious diseases which afflict more than an occasional cat. (Skin ailments are discussed in Chapter V.)

A sick cat usually makes the fact obvious by several physical signs as well as by its behavior. The cat's coat and eyes are remarkably sensitive indices to its state of health. The fur of a healthy cat is smooth and glossy; when a cat is ill the fur becomes rough, dull, lifeless—unthrifty, as it's sometimes called. This change can take place with dramatic swiftness. In feline distemper, for instance, which strikes hard and fast, the quality of the coat may go from one extreme to another in a few days. Normally, a cat's eyes are one of its most beautiful features—glistening and alert. If they become red-rimmed or watery, if they develop a discharge, or if the third eyelid, or nictitating membrane, suddenly becomes visible across the surface of the eye, it means the cat is ailing somewhere.

A cat's nose, on the other hand, is not a reliable index of

its well-being. One used to hear that if a cat or dog's nose was hot and dry, it meant the animal had a fever and that, conversely, a cold, wet nose was a sign of perfect health. It would be just about as accurate to say that anyone who sweated in an overheated room or after playing three sets of tennis was running a temperature. A cat can have a wet nose and be feverish or feel perfectly fit with a dry one. Your suspicions about the cat's health would be justifiable only if you couldn't account for a dry nose in terms of outside temperature and humidity or the cat's activity.

Vomiting, diarrhea and constipation are obvious signs, of course, as they are in humans and other animals, that all is not normal. For purposes of rough diagnosis, vomiting might be separated into two types: the real thing and simple regurgitation. Cats seem to have a special penchant for giving back certain things they have swallowed, like grass, their own hair, or the indigestible portions of rodents eaten whole. They are also likely to return food they have eaten too fast, food that is too cold, or a food for which they have an individual intolerance. Some cats spit up frequently, some rarely. Cat owners usually come to recognize this sort of vomiting as an individual idiosyncracy in their pets and can guess to what it may be attributed.

Real vomiting, on the other hand, is quite different and may indicate any one of several ailments. If a cat gags and vomits repeatedly, if it seems wretched, if the vomit is yellowish, greenish, blood-streaked or foul-smelling, there is no doubt the cat is sick. The diagnosis should be made by a vet, but the cat owner can help him by being able to give an accurate description of the vomited material itself as well as any other signs of distress the cat may show.

Like regurgitation, both diarrhea and constipation may have a cause as simple as sudden change in diet. The cat isn't sick; its insides are simply thrown off stride temporarily. However, if either condition lasts for several days, if the cat is off its feed or shows any additional symptoms, some more serious reason should be suspected. Hairballs and other obstructions, worms, and faulty diet are common causes of constipation. Intestinal irritation, infection, poisoning, worms again and several viral diseases may be responsible for the diarrhea. It's easy to check routinely on the habits of a cat using an indoor pan, not so easy to keep track of one using outdoor facilities. But if you have any cause to suspect trouble in the intestinal department, you should make every effort to observe a bowel movement and be especially alert to other clues the cat may give, such as hunching and straining, crying, dragging its rear end along the floor or acting sluggish.

The two commonest internal ailments cats suffer from—hairballs and worms—are, in a sense, penalties of domestication. Hairballs do not seem to be a problem for the wild cats, possibly because of differences in diet and environment, and although wild animals are certainly not immune to parasites, they rarely are exposed to such concentrations of them as domestic animals may be.

Hairballs are peculiar to cats and are the result of their methods of self-cleaning and grooming. A cat's tongue is sandpapery rough; when the cat licks itself the loose hair on its coat sticks to the tongue and is swallowed. Normally, the cat will either regurgitate a swallowed wad of hair or uneventfully pass it along and out the other end. However, the system often breaks down for house cats, especially for longhairs. They can't roam in the country where rolling, climbing trees and slithering through underbrush would help get rid of a lot of loose hair, and some owners don't help out by brushing them regularly. As a result, they swallow more hair than they can get rid of, and it accumulates, often in unbelievable quantities, in their intestines or stomachs. Quite often veterinarians have to surgically remove hairballs as big as tennis balls, or thick ropes of hair perhaps a foot long.

A cat with problem-size hairballs loses its appetite, may become constipated and grows increasingly thinner. If the mass of hair in its interior hasn't grown too large, the cat can be helped to pass it along with regular doses of mineral oil— one or two teaspoons daily for not longer than a week. If this treatment fails, better consult a vet. Mineral oil, incidentally, is the only oil useful as a lubricant because it is not digested; vegetable oils, which are sometimes mistakenly used in its place, are broken down in the body and absorbed. However, the very property that makes a few doses of mineral oil valuable makes prolonged dosing with it inadvisable; if it is given daily over long periods of time, it can cause deficiencies of the fat-soluble vitamins.

Though faithful brushing of a cat is the most effective way to prevent hairballs, proper diet, too, can impede their growth. A diet that includes plenty of bulk such as fibrous vegetables, spinach, lettuce and grass helps carry off the hair.

Internal parasites, particularly worms of several species and many varieties, make life unnecessarily miserable for countless cats. In fact, it has been estimated that at least ten per cent of the puppies and kittens born each year die from the effects of parasitism. Many people are inclined to shrug off worms as a sort of inevitable burden cats must suffer, or to think they are of little consequence. They are completely wrong in both instances. It is relatively easy to prevent domestic pets from becoming heavily infested with worms, and if by unhappy chance they are infested it's usually not hard to get rid of their parasites. Worms are not to be taken lightly. An infestation can be large enough to kill a cat. Less dramatic but nonetheless serious damage is the lowered disease resistance, retarded growth and general ill health of a cat with worms. When you consider that forty hookworms can suck an ounce of a cat's blood in twenty-four hours, you have some idea of what an ordinary infestation of several hundred can do in a matter of weeks. Finally, it should be remembered that a cat does not always carry its burden alone. Some varieties of worms may also prey on human beings.

To control worms efficiently, one should know which are the commonest varieties, and what their methods of operation are. Cats seem to be susceptible to considerably fewer kinds of these parasites than dogs are. Those most often encountered in felines are: roundworms (or ascarids), hookworms, and tapeworms of three or more varieties.

Intestinal roundworms are whitish or cream-colored and may grow to be as much as eight inches long. Their eggs are laid inside the host, passed out in a bowel movement, and can live for years, waiting for a new host to happen by. A cat may pick them up on its feet or coat from which it unwittingly licks them off, or it may swallow them in contaminated food or water. In the cat's stomach, the egg is liberated from its shell, becomes a larva and moves to the intestines where it grows. Next, it bores through the lining of the intestines, enters the blood stream and travels to the lungs. The irritation it causes there makes the cat cough it up and swallow it again, thus returning it to the intestines to reproduce and live to a contented old age.

There are three varieties of hookworms that pester cats, but all share the same life cycle, slightly different and somewhat more sinister than that of the roundworm. Hookworm eggs again are laid within the host and passed in the stool. The eggs then go through three larval stages, waiting for their host. They may be accidentally swallowed, inhaled or, most horrid of all, can bore through the animal's skin. If the latter takes place, they migrate to the lungs, are coughed up and swallowed. In any case, their final destination is the cat's intestines where in three or four weeks they are sufficiently mature to lay new eggs. Hookworms are far smaller than roundworms; their usual length is half to three-quarters of an inch and they are about as big around as a pin.

Life is more complicated for a tapeworm, though due to the prevalence of fleas, not complicated enough. Tapeworms need an intermediate host to complete their life cycle; for the commonest variety, fleas and biting lice provide it. Tapeworms are segmented and the eggs are contained in the final segments of the parent. These segments break off and pass out of the anal opening to become a meal for flea and louse larvae. On this diet the larvae develop into adults, infest a cat, and quite often get swallowed by the cat which liberates the still-living tapeworm egg in the cat's insides.

With a working knowledge of the life cycle of these worms, it is easier to interpret the apparently unrelated symptoms of worminess a cat may exhibit. Occasional coughing and gagging may point to roundworms or hookworms; anemia (to which pale gums are the tip-off) is more likely to suggest hookworms; sluggishness, poor appetite, rough coat, bowel irregularities and, rarely, fits are some of the other symptoms of all three varieties. Animals seldom pass roundworms or hookworms in their stools, so no clues are to be found there, except in a microscopic analysis which will show the eggs. However, the tapeworm segments are frequently visible to the naked eye on the surface of a bowel movement or clinging to the cat's hair; but conversely a stool analysis is not a definite test for tapeworm since the eggs aren't laid in the host.

The most important thing for the owner of a cat to bear

in mind is that parasitism is a gradual process. A cat that seems well one day is not sick the next because of worms. Quite possibly, it has worms too, but sudden symptoms are due to some other ailment. Often a cat with a virus infection vomits, coughs up a worm, and its owner assumes the worm caused the vomiting. If, on this mistaken assumption, he undertakes to worm the cat at this moment, he may quite possibly kill it.

Kittens are born with roundworms more often than not. If roundworms infest the mother they can, in their passage through the bloodstream, penetrate the placenta and eventually the embryo kitten. Since newborn kittens haven't the resistance of older cats, a heavy infestation can kill them before the owner even realizes it exists. Obvious symptoms of worminess in kittens are: pot bellies, poor coats and diarrhea. The easiest way to prevent wormy kittens, of course, is to make sure the mother is free of worms. Even so, it is always a good idea to have a stool test made when the kittens are four to six weeks old, to make sure they aren't harboring any strays.

The treatment for internal parasites is such a vast subject that there may even be a textbook on it. Present medical feeling is that it is not something that should routinely be undertaken by the layman. Although there is now a drug to kill roundworms which is effective and safe for home use, the drugs most effective against hookworms and tapeworms are so potent that careless use of them can also kill the host. The wisest course is to discuss the situation with a veterinarian and follow his instructions to the letter.

Although treatment in most cases is better left to the veterinarian, prevention of worms is squarely the responsibility of the cat's owner. It rests simply upon good sanitation and some dietary supervision. Fecal matter contaminated with roundworm eggs and larvae is the primary source of roundworm and hookworm infestation, so it is important to change a cat's pan frequently, dispose of its contents completely and clean it thoroughly. Strict flea control is the best way to guard against tapeworm infestation. Country cats sometimes pick up other varieties of tapeworm by eating baby rabbits, squirrels or rodents which act as intermediate hosts for the parasites, so it is a good idea to discourage these meals if you can. Regular grooming and clean bedding are such obvious fundamentals of proper hygiene that I almost hesitate to mention them. Finally, good diet comes up yet again as having an important bearing on parasite control. It has been demonstrated quite clearly that deficiencies in diet lower an animal's resistance to parasites. Garlic mashed into a cat's daily ration has a hoary and undeserved reputation as a home preventive of roundworms. Though a steady diet of garlic may make an occasional roundworm with a sensitive nose seek other living quarters, the probability is that it merely serves to make the cat's owner wish the cat had other living quarters.

Coccidiosis is caused by a different sort of parasite, the protozoan or one-celled coccidia. It seems to afflict young cats in particular and is widely prevalent. Like worms, coccidia are usually picked up on a kitten's feet or coat from contaminated feces or water, and make their way to the small intestine where they destroy considerable tissue. The most pronounced symptom of the disease is a bloody diarrhea which usually can be diagnosed promptly with the aid of a stool test. Proper medical treatment can clear up coccidiosis quickly.

Of the more serious diseases to which cats are susceptible, by far the most devastating is the dread cat distemper. In medical circles, this is now usually called panleucopenia, but it may also be called feline infectious enteritis, or by as many other names as a cat has fleas. Veterinarians prefer the first name, because it is a medically accurate description of the disease—pan meaning all, leuco meaning white blood cells and penia meaning absence of, and also because distemper has come to be mistakenly associated in the minds of many people with madness or rabies, with which it hasn't the slightest connection. Fortunately, there is now a vaccine which gives excellent protection against panleucopenia, and no one who loves his cat should fail to provide it. The shot, or shots, are usually given to kittens when they are about eight weeks old.

Infectious panleucopenia is caused by a very small virus that wreaks terrible havoc in a cat's body in an unbelievably short time. It is highly contagious and usually occurs in epizootics—the animal equivalent of epidemics. In this connection, one of the nastier characteristics of the disease is manifested. Panleucopenia appears to be seasonal, but instead of following a clear pattern, it occurs most often when there is a new generation of susceptible cats in an area. For instance, in New England, where there are many spring litters of kittens, the usual time for an outbreak is July and August when there will be a large population of young cats.

The incubation period is four to ten days, after which symptoms appear so suddenly and multiply so swiftly that a cat seemingly well in the morning may be dead by night. A delay of even a few hours in getting medical help for an infected cat can mean the difference between life and death.

When the virus material of panleucopenia invades the body, it establishes itself within the cells of some vital organ where it multiplies with great rapidity, and after destroying these cells moves on to others. The viruses swarm through body tissue, turning the bone marrow to a sort of mush and simultaneously attacking the intestines, lymph glands, and even the kidneys, liver and spleen.

The resulting symptoms are multiple and, unfortunately, may be confused with symptoms of other diseases. Usually, the first is the cat's refusal to eat, coupled with a sudden and tremendous rise in temperature—to 106 or 107 degrees. There may be both diarrhea and vomiting. The cat's coat becomes spiky and lifeless, and the cat itself becomes very weak. The action of the virus dehydrates the animal so swiftly and completely that it seems to shrink to a bag of bones but, though it acts thirsty, often hanging its head over the water dish, it usually refuses to drink; if it does drink, the water is soon vomited.

I have heard all sorts of home treatments recommended for panleucopenia, ranging from frequent nips of brandy to homeopathic remedies. Current medical opinion, however, favors prompt use of an antiserum, backed up by transfusions, forced fluids and one of the broad-spectrum antibiotics to fight secondary infection. According to recent studies, the mortality rate declined from 90 per cent in untreated cases to 10 per cent in cases where antiserum and aureomycin were used. If the cat survives the first few days of the disease, which has a course of six to nine days, its chances for recovery are good. However, the poor soul has been as sick as a cat is ever likely to be, and convalescence may be slow. A super-nourishing high protein diet and plenty of fluids will help it along considerably.

Although a cat that has recovered from panleucopenia becomes immune to further attacks, the virus can linger around the premises for an incredible length of time, and the most rigid sanitary precautions should be taken to avoid spreading it to other hapless cats. Anyone who has been nursing the sick cat can carry the virus on his clothes or shoes and, of course, the cat's bed and immediate surroundings are likely to be loaded with disease organisms. No other cat, unless it has been inoculated, should be allowed in the house for several months afterward.

One of the more recently recognized feline diseases is infectious anemia; there is still much to be learned about it, and cat owners often don't realize it is present until it has reached a critical stage. In this disease, viruslike organisms attack and destroy the animal's red blood cells, causing anemia, depression, loss of appetite and weight and, sometimes, at the beginning, a high fever. It hasn't been definitely established how infectious anemia is transmitted, but researchers suspect that a large proportion of the cat population may have it in a latent form. They have come to this conclusion because it so often follows another illness or seems to be triggered by some stress factor. Blood transfusions, certain antibiotics and a highly nourishing diet seem so far the most effective ways to treat it.

Respiratory disease in cats is a relatively new field for research, and to make the subject more confusing to the average person, such inaccurate terms as "common cold," "sniffles" and "coryza" still linger on. However, the main fact of interest to a cat owner is that the highly contagious feline respiratory diseases are caused by viruses; of these, the most common is what is currently called feline pneumonitis. A person looking at the cat would probably say it had a bad cold. The cat sneezes persistently (spraying the air with infective droplets), its eyes run, it seems generally depressed and wretched. Because its sense of smell is temporarily destroyed, it loses interest in eating and soon becomes thin and rundown. It usually runs a temperature. If the cat is given no treatment, the illness may drag on for weeks or months and, in the cat's debilitated condition, secondary infections are likely to develop. Prompt treatment with the proper antibiotics, supplementary vitamins, plenty of fluids and a high quality diet can shorten its course enormously.

The symptoms of rabies, a horrible virus disease which attacks the central nervous system of animals and humans, have already been described. However, even though it is invariably fatal to animals, it deserves a few more words here because of its danger to human beings. Although rabies has been greatly curtailed in dogs by compulsory inoculation in many states, similar preventive measures are not always taken with cats, and prevention of the disease in wild animals is, naturally, almost impossible. A survey made by the Department of Agriculture showed that between 1938 and 1955, 113,484 cases had been reported in dogs and 6,514 in cats. That is an appreciable drop; but nevertheless, of the domestic and farm animals susceptible to rabies, cats came after dogs and cattle in contracting it most frequently. Rabies is transmitted by the bite of an infected animal, and the incubation period may last from two weeks to several months. The symptoms in cats are hoarseness, loss of appetite, inability to swallow, and a tendency to hide in dark places. It is this last symptom that makes domestic cats dangerous; they are likely to take refuge under a bed or in a closet and suddenly leap out and viciously attack whoever comes near them. Stay away from any cat that behaves peculiarly, no matter whether it is a stranger or a beloved pet, and get professional reinforcements as quickly as possible.

Urinary calculi is a metabolic disease, fairly recently recognized and still the subject of much medical controversy. It is sometimes called kidney stones. They cause a great deal of pain to a great many badly fed cats. With that last sentence, I am wading straight into the controversy. Authorities do seem to agree, though they differ on the fine points, that diet plays a major part in the development of calculi. The mineral requirement of cats still is not definitely known, in spite of the intensive laboratory research being done, and the current belief is that a diet which contains a disproportionately high quantity of minerals, such as fish bones, has a good deal to do with the formation of these tiny stones in the kidneys or bladder. It is also suspected that a deficiency in Vitamin A may be a factor. Male cats, because of their physiological structure, have more trouble with calculi than females; it is difficult for the stones to work their way out of the urethra, where they may accumulate to form a stoppage. But for cats of either sex, kidney stones are a painful affliction, as an owner can readily tell by the cat's straining and crying when it tries to urinate. If the stones are severe, there may be blood in the urine. A urinanalysis will confirm the presence of calculi, and treatment for them —principally a dietary regime—should be prescribed by a veterinarian.

One of the most striking signs of progress in feline medicine is the new need for feline geriatrics, and in this branch of medicine enormous strides have been taken. As more and more cats live into old age—twelve to eighteen years, perhaps —they fall heir to many of the old-age troubles that beset human beings. Vascular disease, attributable mainly to chronic obesity, as it is in humans, is a major problem; tumors and kidney disease are others. Present-day drugs and treatments can do remarkable things, not only to prolong life but to make old age more comfortable for animals. Naturally, there is a point beyond which medicine and even the most devoted home nursing can't go. When this point is reached and a pet is no longer able to enjoy life or is in pain or discomfort most of the time, the only humane thing to do is to have it put to sleep. This is an agonizing decision for an owner to face, but if one is objective, one realizes that the emotions that make it so painful are purely selfish. And, surely, when the alternatives are to watch a creature struggle through the final stages of agony or to see it go quietly to sleep without a moment's fear or pain, as it can with modern drugs, there can be no choice in anyone's mind.

Part II

Cats in General

Chapter VIII

What Cats Are Made of

One of the many fascinations of the cat is its suggestion of wildness. While most breeds of dogs have undergone such transmutations that some hardly seem like animals at all, but more like a peculiar kind of human wearing a fur coat, the

117

cat seems to have come out of the jungles of prehistory quite intact. Looking into the eyes of a cat, one gains a sense of contact with something elemental. Look into the eyes of a spaniel and what do you see? Nothing that gives one this particular thrill, I'm sure. Carl Van Vechten expressed my feeling about the wildness of cats succinctly in the title of his classic, *A Tiger in the House.*

Having formed this notion of cats, I became curious to know if there was anything to it, or if it were merely a bit of personal romanticism. I wondered if my tiger-striped Minnie is really the miniature wildcat she seems to be, or as distant from her wild ancestors as the most respectable dachshund is from the wolf or the dingo. This question, in turn, aroused my curiosity about the whole cat tribe, the felines, or *Felidae,* as they are properly called. Everything I have since learned about them has enhanced the feeling that my first instincts about Minnie's associations were not far off. In spirit she may indeed be close to the beginnings of feline time, and in substance she differs in little more than size from such dramatic relatives as the tiger and the lynx. In more than one or two cases, Minnie and certain relatives would be kissing cousins should they ever meet.

Cats and dogs and, in fact, all the carnivores of today have a common progenitor: a small weasel-like animal named Miacis whose bones, of which a few now repose in museums, are in the range of forty million years old. From Miacis were evolved civet cats, catty little beasts very much like the civets which still survive. But while some civets remained civets and nothing more, others turned into cats, true felines in every respect. This happened in the early Oligocene period, about thirty million years ago. Of these prehistoric cats, one branch of the family—the Hoplophoneus branch—made a fatal genetic error, though it doubtless seemed a good idea at the time. It evolved the enormous canine teeth typified by Smilodon, the fearsome saber-toothed tiger. Though the saber-toothed cats survived as late as twenty thousand years ago, they finally succumbed, perhaps because of overspecialization, leaving the field to those cats that had chosen versatility over heavy armament. Modern cats, then, are not, as many people assume, direct descendants of saber-tooths, but cousins whose families branched very early in cat history.

The early cats were of many species and ranged in size from miniatures no bigger than the house cat to giants three times the size of today's tiger, yet it is believed that should one of them reappear it would be very much like our familiar modern cats.

Perhaps it was the cat's early perfection that has allowed it to remain so unchanged. Brian Vesey-Fitzgerald, an Englishman who has written studiously about cats, calls the cat tribe "the most highly developed, the most beautifully perfect of all the Carnivora," and quotes the naturalist, St. George Mivart: ". . . the cat has padded feet which make no sound in movement; muscles of enormous power and bulk in proportion to its size and attached to bones adjusted to each other at such angles as to form the most complete system of springs and levers for propelling the body . . . the claws are sharper and curved into strong hooks more than in any other animal, and by action of special muscles are withdrawn under sheathlike pads, that they may escape injury and wear. . . . No teeth are better fitted for their work, the great canines for tearing, and the scissor-like premolars for shearing off lumps of flesh. . . . In the eye, the fibres of the iris, opening to the widest extent, expand the pupil to full circle, admitting the darkness of night, and by rapid contraction shut off all excess of blinding light at midday."

These majestic words are true not only of lions and tigers,

119

but of the pretty little ten-pound striped beast named Minnie that first inspired me to read them. As I watch her kneading my lap into a more satisfactory texture upon which to fold herself, springs, levers and all, I am filled with a new respect. She settles down to rest and think her Oligocene thoughts, leaving me to think my twentieth century ones, and marvel that even to this extent the twain should meet.

Zoologists have devised a system of classifying animals with a series of names which starts out broadly and ends so specifically that it pinpoints a unique set of beasts. It is as seemingly simple as that childhood game of addressing a letter to Mary Jones, No. 1 Main Street, Middletown, Whatever State, U.S.A., Northern Hemisphere, Earth, Solar System, Milky Way Galaxy, and so on. Using this system in reverse, my cat might be located as follows: Class *Mammalia*, Order *Carnivora*, Super Family *Aeluroidea*, Family *Felidae*, Genus *Felis*, species *catus*, sub-species tiger-striped, variety grocery store, name Minnie. However, there is grave doubt that Minnie would get a letter so addressed. Things are not quite that tidy in zoology. There might be no argument about Minnie's family name, or perhaps about her genus (If Minnie happened to be an ocelot there could indeed be argument about her classification), but when it came to species the postman might claim that Minnie is not *catus* but *domestica*, and deliver the letter instead to one of her cousins among the European wild cats. Since Minnie wouldn't particularly want a letter, even if it came from Darwin himself, and since the arguments rest upon points as fine as one of her whiskers, I don't intend to go into it any further. I bring it up only to explain why it is that some authors flatly call house cats *Felis domestica* while others just as flatly call them *Felis catus*.

It also explains why one cannot say positively just how many species of cats exist today. The number depends on whether you put some of them in a species or in a sub-species. Probably it is safe to say that there are between fifty and sixty kinds of cats, provided you do not say it in the presence of a scientist with strong views on exact nomenclature in feline classification. Unhappily, it is even safer to say that whatever the number of species now on earth, the number is likely to be decreased. Cats in the wild have held their own remarkably well, but civilization is inexorable in narrowing their range.

Felines tolerate all sorts of terrain, from snowy mountains to forests and deserts, but in general they are warm-weather creatures and the greatest number of species occur in the tropics and semi-tropics. Before mankind began to take over the earth rather than share it—only a couple of hundred years ago in fact—there were felines galore in every part of the world except the Arctic, Antarctic, Australia, New Zealand, Madagascar and Polynesia. However, man, in the course of his take-over, saw fit to all but wipe out many wild animals, including several sorts of cats: the North American puma, for instance, the Barbary lynx, the European wildcat and the Indian lion, to name but a few. African lions are still doing pretty well—whether there are plenty depends upon your point of view—but it seems that the continent once teemed with them. Roman records refer to incredible numbers of captive lions; as many as six hundred in a single display in the arena. Now there may not be that many in hundreds of square miles of their former range.

North America has fewer kinds of cats than do warmer zones, chiefly the lynx and the puma, but it once had these in abundance. The abundance is illustrated by an episode which took place in Pennsylvania only a little over two hundred years ago. In 1760 a group of hunters organized an animal drive and in one day, and in a fairly small area, killed

121

41 pumas (or panthers as they called them), 114 lynx, and hundreds of other animals. One outcome of the slaughter was to enrage the local Indians who disapproved of mass killing. Another was to make panther-skin suits suddenly fashionable. The fashion was as suddenly dropped when the Indians, to show their displeasure, took to attacking any white man caught wearing one. Most eastern states offered bounties on lynx and puma until fairly recently. The puma gave up first. By 1850, for instance, it was believed extinct in Massachusetts, and soon it was gone from the East except in Florida. The lynx, better known as the bobcat in the United States, did better and even now bobcats may show up any place where there are deep woods.

But whether one speaks of puma or house cat, or any of the feline family in any part of the world, the distinctive features of cattiness prove to be remarkably consistent and to fit all cats for a special way of life—that of the solitary hunter.

To begin with, the springs and levers that St. George Mivart mentions, the bones and muscles of felines, are put together in such a way as to make them perhaps the most flexible of four-footed animals. One result is the cat's great repertoire of fascinatingly graceful postures, whose purpose is not aesthetic, but functional and lethal. The cat's litheness gives it the speed, agility and power to bring down its prey. It can spring like an arrow from a taut bow. As an added dividend, the cat's suppleness allows it to scratch every part of its anatomy. Cat teeth are also distinctive and are one of the features by which zoologists classify felines, but it is the feet of cats that are most interestingly unique.

All cats have retractable claws. The secret is a strong ligament, like an elastic band, that pulls back the final toe bone to which the claw is attached. In the front foot the bone and claw fold back into a sheath which is beside the next-to-final bone. In the hind foot the sheath is above the bone. Cats stretch their claws not only to sharpen them, but to exercise the retractile ligament. All cats normally have five front toes and four hind toes (the fifth is rudimentary), arranged around a central pad that is hairless and sensitive; like those of human beings, the cat's palms becomes moist with excitement. Only the toes of the cat touch the ground. What one might assume is the cat's ankle is actually its heel, an arrangement that gives the cat extra bounce when needed. Bounce is, in fact, the characteristic gait of a cat in a hurry. A cat has numerous gaits to choose from. It can walk, trot, stalk, creep, slink, swagger, amble or pussy-foot, in fact do everything except stamp; but in full gallop it bounces like an India rubber ball, and in a sprint can outdistance most animals twice its size.

Like many other animals, felines, including domestic toms, have anal glands. These are small sacs under the tail. The substance they secrete is objectionably smelly to humans, but to other cats this musky stuff is essential to their love life. It assures that despite their solitary way of life they will find each other at the proper time. Like dogs, cats leave what used to be euphemistically called calling cards. Civet cats—which are not felines but are closely related—are particularly noted for their musk. The Indian civet, or rasse, is a small, prettily marked creature that the Javanese keep not only as a pet, but to milk of its musk, which they value as an ingredient of perfume. (True musk comes from a gland of the musk deer, but several creatures secrete a similar substance.) Another civet, exotically named the zibeth, can emit what must be one of the world's most powerful smells, so strong that even dogs are overcome by the stench. Perversely, dogs love to chase zibeths above all else.

On the other hand the fur of cats is practically odorless. Felines have sebacious glands which provide oil to coat the hair, but the oil has no smell detectable to the human nose. Some say that the fur of a lion has a faint scent something like honey, and it seems to me that this is approximately how a house cat smells, with a suggestion of milk and sweet grass thrown in.

Cat tails come in all lengths, from the stump of the bobcat to the elegantly long and wavy type worn by the lion, but there are more long-tailed than short-tailed cats. The Manx cat has no tail at all, not even a stump; however, the Manx is not a species, but a mutation of the domestic cat. As in dogs the feline tail is a most important means of expression. But the vocabulary of the cat's tail is as different from the dog's as a miaouw from a bark.

The tongue of all cats is prickly and serves to rasp bits of juicy meat from bones; it is useful too in cleaning and smoothing fur. Even on a house cat the prickles can be felt; those few people who have been licked by a lion compare it to being wiped with wet sandpaper.

The vocal accomplishments of cats—large or small—probably surpass those of all other animals, with the possible exception of the human and the monkey. A cat may not be able to sing the "Star Spangled Banner," but it can yodel its own music in a way no human throat can duplicate. The vocal repertoire of the cat is so wide, from the small, questioning *mee* of a house cat asking about supper, to the scream of a panther and the snarl of a tiger, that it is almost impossible to describe. Most enchanting to those who like cats is the purr. It is not a voice sound made by the larynx, but comes from the vibration of the soft palate which, in cats, is as long as the hard palate. The less attractive human equivalent is a snore. Lions, tigers, leopards and, as far as I can discover, all the others purr as sweetly as any house cat, though the bigger the cat the grander the scale of the vibration.

Feline whiskers and eyebrows are long and tough and grow out of bulblike follicles that are highly sensitive. The whiskers themselves have no feeling, of course, but any pressure on them is transmitted to the follicle so that the whiskers serve as organs of touch.

The hide of the cat is tactile all over, as anyone knows who has ever observed the pleasure of a cat as it is stroked. Each hair follicle has a nerve and muscle by which the cat can make its hair stand on end at appropriate moments. This device, allowing an animal to look bigger than it is, is not exclusive to the cat. Many mammals can do it. Man, who cannot, makes up for the deficiency with such inventions as the bustle, the padded shoulder and the raccoon coat.

Another trademark of the feline is its eyes, which are adapted to seeing in dim light. No animal, not even the cat, can see in total blackness, as is demonstrated by the fact that cave-dwelling fish and toads have given up eyes altogether. But the outdoor night world is never totally black. Human vision is actually quite good at night, but the cat's is even better. In the cat's eye reception of dim light is enhanced not only by enormous distention of the pupil, but by a special reflecting device, the *tapetum lucidum*, underlying the retina. The tapetum is a mirror-like surface that throws light back onto the retina and accounts for the way a cat's eyes shine like highway beacons when a beam of light strikes them. The eyeshine of cats is not uniform; it varies with an individual's eye color, with the angle of the light striking it, and the opening of the pupil. The reflected shine may be pinkish, greenish, bluish or golden. It may change when an animal becomes excited.

The eyes of the jaguar have been described as glowing like

great balls of fire, and Siamese also have a red reflection. Again, eyeshine is not unique in cats—the eyes of bears shine deep red and those of deer glow orange-yellow—but it has given rise to much of the mysticism and myth surrounding the cat. One of the reasons the Egyptians identified cats with the moon goddess is thought to be the waxing and waning of the pupil and the eerie moon-like glow of the tapetum. Before the principle of reflection was understood, there was a popular idea that feline eyes emitted rays of light, a notion that can be linked to the Greek's emanation hypothesis that vision consists of sending out gossamer threads that touch the object perceived.

It has even been said that there are cats which fish at night, crouched by the water in such a way that starlight reflected in their eyes attracts fish, but since I have never crouched by the water in the starlight accompanied by a cat, I am not in a position to say whether this is true.

In dim light only the rod cells of the retina function, and rod cells do not register color. At twilight the human eye sees only various shades of gray. The retina of the cat has a predominance of rod cells. It was once thought that cats were completely color-blind. The current theory is that the eye of the cat is able to receive some color stimuli, but that the brain does not utilize the information.

In daylight, feline vision, like that of other nocturnal animals, is considerably poorer than normal human vision, in the sense that the cat's eye lacks the acuity of the human eye. Acuity is measured by the ability to distinguish a small object from its background. In a comparison of the vision of domestic cats with the vision of human beings, the ratio is about five to one. In other words, a man can pick out a small object at five times the distance at which it is discernible to the cat. Or, conversely, a pinpoint visible to a man at a certain distance must be five times as large to be visible to a cat at the same distance. Even so, cats see better than some other nocturnal animals. Opossums have only half their visual acuity and rats less than one-fifth. Cats compensate to some extent for poor vision by their quick response to movement. Until recently it was thought that cats were also poor at distinguishing form; that is, in perceiving the difference between, say, a square and a triangle. New tests have shown that domestic cats can be taught to pick out patterns that differ very slightly indeed.

Not all felines, incidentally, have pupils that contract to the typical vertical slit. In a few species the pupil becomes oval or contracts to a pinpoint.

Because a cat's senses are specialized so differently from the senses of human beings, it is difficult to imagine just how things seem to a cat. Taste and smell, for instance, are very hard to measure in another human being, let alone in an animal whose subjective world of sensation is so far from our own experience. The behavior of both cats and dogs suggests that they live in a world in which smell is a very important component. They perhaps receive as much information from smells as humans do from vision. (We have lost our sense of smell, it has been said, because we have raised our noses so far above the ground. Even before that, we sacrificed some of our sensitivity to smell when we took our noses out of the water. Water is the best conductor of the particles which comprise odors, and fish have the keenest smelling organs of any of the vertebrate beasts. In land animals, to this day, noses work better when they are wet and that is why dogs and cats frequently moisten them with their tongues.)

Cats seem to make their decisions about food by smelling it before they taste it, but they are of course perfectly able to taste as well. The tongue of the cat is well supplied with taste buds. It seems, though, to have no specific receptor for the taste of sweetness. Three kinds of taste receptors have been identified in cats: those which respond to sour, those which respond to salty and sour, and those which respond to sour and bitter. Because people dislike any of these tastes when they are too strong, one feels that the cat must have a bad taste in its mouth if these are the only impressions it gets. This, of course, isn't so. Meat is a mixture of salty, sour, bitter and sweet tastes. To a cat a piece of steak may not have the slight sweetness we detect, but tastes fine nonetheless.

In hunting, cats rely more on vision and hearing, while dogs rely more on smell. In cats, dogs and many other animals, the smell of members of its own species seems to hold many messages, particularly of a romantic or challenging nature. Cats in the wild use scent posts, a particular tree or bush on which they spray and which they visit regularly. Everyone has seen a dog investigate a lamp post much as though it were reading a fifty-word telegram before deciding what answer to file, and it is likely that cats are just as accomplished in deciphering the code. Cats seem to recognize each other's sex from quite a distance and are understandably puzzled upon encountering an altered cat.

Cats can distinguish people by smell and it is only courteous upon being introduced to a cat to extend a finger for it to sniff. Zoo keepers who handle the kittens of zoo cats are careful to wear gloves so that the kitten will not be contaminated by human smell, and so made unwelcome to the mother. Laboratory tests on house cats have shown that before a kitten's eyes open it responds to the smell of its nest. If the nest is cleaned up and new bedding put down, the kitten shows by its crying and creeping that it is upset.

Tests on dogs have shown that where a human being perceives a mélange of smells as just one big smell, a dog can analyze its components much as a musician can distinguish the notes in a musical chord. It is likely that cats can do the same. As unscientific but perhaps significant evidence of the cat's sense of smell, I submit that the opening of a can of fish in the kitchen is enough to wake Minnie out of a sound sleep in an upstairs room. (It isn't the sound of the can-opener; opening a can of soup produces no effect on her.)

The feline preference in smells is different from the canine in ways that befit their differences in personality and way of life. Dogs like good, strong, ripe smells and are indifferent to catnip. Cats enjoy quite a number of flower smells. They tour a garden with apparent appreciation and are apt to raise havoc with living-room flower arrangements. They like perfume and hand lotion.

This is not to suggest that the aesthetics of smell are the same for cats and people. All felines love to roll in the manure of herbiverous creatures, and the recipe for a concoction used in baiting lynx traps is stupefying: mix oily fish, minced mice, musk glands of mink, weasel or muskrat, and meat scraps. Grind in meat chopper. Put aside to ripen for a week or so. A tablespoon of this stuff, it is guaranteed, will bring cats of all kinds from miles around.

The smell of the catnip plant, *Nepeta cataria*, has a special effect on all felines that has yet to be explained. It seems to be slightly intoxicating and perhaps aphrodisiac to cats, but leaves dogs and human beings cold. Circus trainers were the first to discover its power to reduce a hostile lion to a state of silly bliss. This feline weakness is exploited by the U. S. Government which grows catnip for use in predator control: that is, in trapping puma and bobcats in areas where they bother ranchers. It takes a ton of catnip to produce a pint of the essential oil, but this extract is so powerful that a few drops on a piece of cotton will lure pumas to the spot for as long as six months.

My mother used to say that anyone who caught every nuance of what was going on "had ears like a lynx." Cats and many other animals have long been credited with having much better hearing than human beings. It is now thought, however, that animal hearing is not necessarily better than human hearing, but rather that animals receive a different range of sound frequency. Recent tests comparing human hearing with that of laboratory animals have given very exact findings on the frequencies each is able to receive.

The mouse can hear a sound up to 95,000 cycles per second; the cat up to 60,000 cycles per second; the white rat up to 40,000 cycles per second; the dog up to 35,000 cycles per second and the human up to 20,000 cycles per second. It is impossible to give an example of what these very high notes sound like because no human has ever heard them. The conversations of mice, for instance, may be carried on in squeaks too high for the human ear, but distinctly audible to cats. In music, the highest notes of a piccolo are around 16,000 cycles. The top piano note is 8,000 cycles.

In hearing low notes, humans outdo cats. We can hear a sound as low as 20 cycles per second, but the cat hears nothing below 62 cycles per second. The hum of a radio when it is turned on but not broadcasting is 60 cycles per second. Within these extreme limits of hearing, each animal has a range in which it can hear best. Above 4,000 cycles the cat's hearing is more sensitive than the human, but for sounds below 500 cycles the cat is inferior.

Frequency, or pitch, is one component of sound. The other is intensity or loudness. There have been no comparative studies on the reception of very tiny sounds, such as the proverbial pin dropping, but in this respect the human ear is so sensitive it is hard to see how any animal could hear more keenly. If the human ear were any keener than it is, we would be disturbed by the sound of molecules moving around us. Cats probably hear as keenly as we do, but no more so.

Lay observers of house cats maintain that most of them like music, particularly the piano and organ. Vesey-Fitzgerald mentions a cat that so adored the organ that it regularily attended musical services in the village church. Beyond this, Mr. Fitzgerald asserts that his cat could distinguish the sound of his automobile from all others—including those of the same make. During the war there were many reports of cats that somehow knew when bombs were imminent or that danger had passed. I have no idea if this is myth or fact. Many people believe it to be true, but have offered no adequate explanation.

The whole question of the mysterious "somehow" by which cats do inexplicable things is vast and maddeningly vague. Much of this kind of cat lore is so mixed up with early superstitious concepts, which made cats the familiars of witches and assigned to them supernatural powers, that one is tempted to skip the whole matter and say flatly that cats have the exact variety of senses human beings possess and nothing more.

Chief among the cat's inexplicable powers is its ability to find its way home over incredible distances. There are countless stories of such instances—some so impossible as to be plain silly—that they are not only a puzzle but a bore. Yet it is beyond dispute that a great many animals—birds, fish and others—make extraordinary journeys, finding their way by means that have not yet been explained. Undoubtedly cats do too. By what means, nobody knows. One way to approach the problem is to determine how they don't do it. One investigator anesthetized cats, so that presumably they neither saw, smelled, heard, felt nor memorized the trip. He carried them far from home and dumped them in strange territory. The cats inevitably turned up. Where that leaves us, I couldn't say.

Chapter IX

The Feline Family

The simplest way to classify the cat tribe is to divide it into three groups, or genera. These are genus *Felis*, encompassing all the small cats; genus *Panthera*, encompassing the large ones; and genus *Acinonyx*, in which the cheetah dwells alone. Some authorities subdivide felines in a much more complex manner, adding several genera, but the taxonomic arguments involved are so technical that to the layman they seem to be distinctions without a difference.

The cheetah is a true cat, but it is the most distinctive of them all. If I were to acquire a wild pet, the cheetah would

132

be the most sensible choice. It is the only cat, other than *Felis domestica*, that can be relied on to stay tame. All the others are considered more or less unpredictable in a strange situation. The temperament of the cheetah is more like that of a dog than a wildcat. It is affectionate, obedient, and cheerfully accepts such disciplines as walking on a leash. A wild animal dealer in New York City reports that he sells a good many of them as pets at around $1,000 apiece.

The cheetah is a long-legged cat with a long tail and a rather bullet-shaped head. Its coat is coarser than most cats'; the color is usually pale gold shading to white underneath, with solid black dots. (In almost all species of felines, individuals vary in shades of color according to habitat; there are pale lions, dark lions, medium lions and so on, so that a description of the color of any species must be general). Dark stripes on the cheetah's cheeks give it a rather sad expression. Its paws are peculiar. The claws are never fully hidden, a fact which led to the mistaken belief that they were not retractable like the claws of other cats. Cheetahs range through Africa, southwest Asia and India. They have been tamed for centuries and the sport of hunting with them is older than falconry. It is said to have originated with Hushing, King of Persia, in 865 B.C. The Mongol emperors took it up in truly royal style; some had as many as a thousand cheetahs in their retinue.

In India cheetahs are still used to hunt deer. The form is to take the cheetah to the field in a car, hooded and leashed like a falcon. When it is released it drops from the car on the side away from the herd, creeps forward and, with a few magnificent leaps, springs upon the prey. After the kill the huntsman rewards the cheetah with a cup of blood.

The cheetah is the fastest living beast. Over a short distance it can easily outrun a race horse. The horse covers twenty-three feet with each stride. The cheetah, thanks to the flexibility of its legs and spine, also covers twenty-three feet in each bound, even though it is a much smaller animal. But while the horse completes two-and-a-half strides per second, the cheetah completes three and a half per second. In each second of a race the cheetah gains twenty-three feet over the horse.

The *Panthera*, or big cats, are of course the lion, the tiger, the jaguar and the leopard. Big cats are fewer in species, and after centuries of war with mankind, scarcer in number than the small cats. The panther, I was surprised to find, does not exist at all. Panther is simply another name for a leopard or a puma, two quite different cats that live in different parts of the world.

The big cats are among the few beasts left on earth capable of killing and consuming a human being. It is perhaps owing to the shuddery thrill of this thought that lions and tigers have always held first place in popular imagination and folklore. Legend attributes quite different personalities to the lion and the tiger, and rightly so. Lions are more gregarious, tigers solitary. Lions live in open country while tigers prefer jungle. Tigers are truly nocturnal. In captivity the lion is hardier and more tractable than the tiger. Universal myth makes the lion the symbol of majesty and the lioness of maternity. Nobility, generosity, courage are the most often celebrated qualities of the lion. To the Chinese Buddhist the lion symbolizes good luck. To the African he may be a totem animal representing a venerated ancestor for whom a part of every kill is left in the field. Where the lion's name is taboo he is addressed as "Sir" or "Brother." Early European legend abounds in helpful and generous lions that spared virgins and assisted questing knights. In addition it was thought that a lion-skin cap could cure deafness or insanity, lion meat cure paralysis, and a lion heart buried under a house avert lightning. Sufferers from hemorrhoids were advised to sit upon a lion's skin.

Mythological tigers, on the other hand, are magical, mysterious and, like werewolves, given to taking on other forms. In India it is thought that the spirits of men killed by a tiger become its servants, warning it of danger and helping it to kill other humans. Tigers are considered to be of a sensitive nature and easily insulted. Sumatrans take care not to speak disrespectfully of tigers and do not travel bareheaded lest a tiger take it as a personal affront. At night Sumatrans will not knock out a firebrand because the sparks are the tiger's eyes. If a tiger must be killed they try to trap it alive in order first to beg its forgiveness. Some Malay people believe that tigers live in a fabulous Tiger Village where the houses are thatched with human hair. All over the Orient various parts of the tiger's anatomy are powerful magic. In Malaya a single tiger whisker knotted into a man's beard is enough to terrify his enemies.

A practical view of the personalities of lions and tigers can be found in the recent accounts of two women who raised them from cubs: Mrs. Martini of New York's Bronx Zoo, and Mrs. Adamson of Kenya, whose book *Born Free* made her pet lioness, Elsa, internationally known.

In both cases these women confounded the experts who had predicted that the cats would become ferocious after they grew up. Mrs. Martini also raised a black leopard, a variety zoo keepers consider the most resolutely hostile of all cats. Even when fully grown, her leopard remained as dependent and affectionate as a house cat. Mrs. Martini trained it to collar and leash. It learned to carry the daily newspaper up the stairs of her apartment house and was upset when there was no delivery. Unlike many cats, it enjoyed riding in an automobile. Mrs. Martini noted with regret that beyond the age of three months a lion, tiger or leopard is no longer a practical pet to keep in an apartment. By that time her pets weighed some twenty pounds, were playful, mischievous, curious and passionately fond of clawing furniture and emptying cupboards. The tigers loved to splash in the bathtub. The lions were enthusiastic greeters, insisting on answering the doorbell. Both purred mightily with pleasure and rolled on their backs to express joy. Mrs. Martini found that far from being fearless, big cats are easily frightened of new things. A puma at the zoo once fainted from fear.

Except for their size, lions and tigers are typical cats. The male lion's mane and fringe, and the tiger's stripes are their only important distinction from other *Felidae*. In both species there is variation in size and coloration. A large male lion may be ten feet from its nose to the tip of its three-foot tail. The biggest Bengal tiger is bigger than the biggest lion. Both lions and tigers commonly weigh between four and five hundred pounds. The lioness and tigress are smaller and considered more dangerous to man.

Zoo-goers sometimes ask which cat—lion or tiger—would be likely to win a fight. This is a contest that zoo-keepers wish to avoid, but it was often staged in the arenas of Rome. Roman records give the palm to the tiger. Tigers are good swimmers and cross wide rivers. Lions generally live in drier country, but enjoy bathing when they get the opportunity.

The gestation period of lions and tigers is a bit over a hundred days, compared to a bit over sixty days for the house cat. At birth the cubs weigh around three pounds. Their infancy and early development are much like that of domestic kittens. Lions are born with a spotted coat which doesn't fade until maturity.

Lions are reported to fast while they are mating. During

a courtship of a week or so the couple retires into the long grass and the male behaves as a devoted and humble suitor, but when they return to the world his attitude changes. He drives the female from her kill and she must wait until he finishes his meal. When the cubs are born the parents part entirely. The male goes off to hunt, sometimes in company with other males. The female may take up with a younger, unmated lioness that acts as an assistant and nursemaid to the cubs.

Movies have made the lion's roar almost as familiar as a cat's meow, but in the early days of African exploration no travel tale was complete without a description of its hair-raising qualities. One awe-struck explorer wrote: "The roar of a lion is both extremely grand and peculiarly striking. It consists at times of a low, deep moaning repeated five or six times, ending in a faintly audible sigh; at other times he startles the forest with loud, deep-toned solemn roars re-peated in quick succession, increasing and then dying away in low, muffled sounds like distant thunder. When a troop roars in concert one takes the lead while others take their parts like persons singing a catch."

Alan Moorehead in his book, *No Room in the Ark*, tells of watching lions at ease in the game parks in Kenya. He saw prides of a dozen or so sunning themselves. Never having been shot at, they were without fear of man and it was possible to drive a car to within five or six yards without rousing them to more than a sleepy stare. "Sometimes," Moorehead wrote, "as we moved slowly along in low gear the young lions, out of curiosity, would come loping all around us. We might almost have reached out and stroked their smooth, clean, yellow backs, and it was odd to think that if you opened the door and stepped out the chances were that you would instantly die. This propinquity was too much for one of our drivers. He closed his eyes and complained that he felt very cold when the lions came close."

Next to the lion and the tiger, the largest cats are the leopard and its South American equivalent, the jaguar. An African leopard of record size, now in the Yale Museum, measured seven feet, eight and five-eighths inches in length and weighed 192 pounds with an empty stomach. There are leopards in almost all of Africa and a large part of Asia. Jaguars range from Argentina to the southwestern United States. Both cats come in many varieties of size, color and markings. All are beautiful and all are regarded as lethal by the people who share their habitat.

Moorehead noted that anywhere in Central Africa a leopard may leap from above and "scalp you with the speed of light." He went on to say, "I found the leopards more alarming than the lions. They seemed to me to be the most beautiful of all the animals, the most lithe and wild. Those I saw—and you don't see very many—were very pale in color, almost silver, and their throats were marked with a circular band of black fur patches that hung like a necklace from the base of their round cat-heads. There is a hair-trigger ferocity about the leopards. . . . Watching through binoculars, one was confronted with two green, glaring lamps that burned directly into one's own eyes. The pupils had the effect of boring into you. No animal, not even the lion, has such an implacable gaze."

Moorehead watched while a small female leopard prowled about a group of gazelle. "They stood and stared at her with wide straining eyes . . . then trotted toward her. They were in an extremity of fear and yet they simply could not bring themselves to run away. It seemed that some kind of mesmerism was at work. Suddenly the leopard got our scent. Then she was up and away like a ballet dancer and the spell was broken."

Wherever it is possible, leopards and jaguars spend much of their lives in trees. The clouded leopard of South East Asia rarely comes to the ground. It is locally called the tree-tiger and has the longest canine teeth of any living cat. The snow-leopard or ounce is slim and lovely, a silvery cat that inhabits the icy heights of central Asia. Black leopards are not a distinct variety but examples of melanism, the result of a latent gene for blackness, and may be born into a litter of normally colored cubs, just as white animals of all kinds show up from time to time.

The jaguar is a heavier, chunkier cat than the leopard. It may weigh as much as three hundred pounds, but most varieties of jaguar are not that large. Their color varies also from pale fawn through reddish tan to almost black. The belly is white. A Jaguar's spots are not solid, but rosettes in fancy patterns. The night cry of the jaguar is deep and hoarse and said to sound like the syllables *pu pu* repeated over and over. Jaguars hang about rivers and are fond of fish and turtles. If necessary a jaguar will plunge in after a turtle, drag it out of the water and scoop the turtle out of its shell with its claws. The jaguar catches fish by a more ingenious means; *i.e.*, fishing with its tail as a lure. A South American river fish, the tambakis, feeds on fruit that falls into the rivers. The jaguar sits by the bank dabbling its tail in imitation of fruit plopping into the water; then swiftly turns and scoops up the fish as they rise. Naturally the number of people who have watched jaguars doing this is limited. However, reports on the jaguar's fishing technique as described by local Indians, who have seen it, have appeared in the writings of explorers and naturalists for many years. Skeptics may refer to an article by E. W. Gudger in the *Journal of Mammology*, Vol. 27, No. 1, (Feb. 1946).

This may be the place to mention that a great many felines fish, and many swim for profit or pleasure. Many of the

South American cats, large and small, depend on fishing for a part of their living. Norwegian wildcats are said to dive into the water after rats. *Felis viverrina* of India is known as the fishing cat. Wildcats have even been discovered swimming several miles out at sea. Just why, no one knows. An example is the account in *The New York Times*, October 15, 1961, of a surprised fisherman named Alvan Weeks who encountered a bobcat swimming three miles offshore near Naples, Florida, and managed to tow it ashore. Gavin Maxwell, in *Ring of Bright Water*, tells of rescuing a young wildcat from the sea off the Scottish coast; a kindness he later regretted, for the kitten, as soon as it was dry, became a most unmanageable house guest. One wonders if these seagoing cats have lost their minds or simply lost their way. If the latter, what has happened to their fabled sense of direction? It shakes one's confidence in feline infallibility.

Most house cats, it is true, are not so enthusiastic about water, but now and then one meets an exception. Ida Mellon, a great cat authority, reports owning a cat "whose insistence on swimming in the laundry tub greatly retarded the progress of the washerwoman."

A type of long-haired domestic cat native to Turkey is notable for its love of water. Even the kittens voluntarily jump into the river for a dip. It seems particularly strange because swimming is even more unbecoming to a long-haired cat than to a plain cat. The different ways in which different cats regard water is the same as in the dog family. Some love swimming and some despise it.

House cats will fish more readily than they will swim, as has been noted by many a goldfish owner, including the one whose cat, Selima, made a fatal slip and thus inspired Gray's famous elegy of condolence. Included in the literature on fishing cats is an account of a memorable night in Asbury

Park, New Jersey, in the year 1898. On a frosty, moonlight night in October, it was reported, vast schools of whitebait came into shore and the shallows were alive with leaping fish. Somehow word reached the town's cats. They arrived en masse on the beach and were seen gathering fish hand over fist, you might say, and some even waded in for more.

Returning to the catalogue of cats, we come now to *Felis concolor*, a big cat known by many names: puma, panther, mountain lion, catamount, varmint, cougar and *el leone*. Because of its even-colored tawny coat it has been taken for a smaller version of the lion, but actually it is more closely allied to the leopard which it resembles in size and build. The puma once reigned over a vast domain, from Canada to Patagonia. In North America it was the ruling predator from coast to coast, but today the remnants of its North American tribe live on only in the wildest parts of Canada, the mountains of the West and the Florida swamps.

The voice of the puma—it is said to scream like a woman in torture—perhaps accounts for its lurid reputation as a man-eater and horse thief. Actually both offenses are rare, though a puma may nab an occasional lamb, calf or foal and so, of course, the stockman is its sworn enemy. The puma seems to be a particularly shy cat and reluctant to meet human beings. On the other hand it has a large bump of curiosity and will track a man through the woods as though it simply wanted to see what he was going to do next. Mistaken identity may account for at least one occasion when a puma attacked a man. The man was sitting by a lake fishing, wearing a raccoon coat turned up about his ears, when a puma landed on him and knocked him flat. When it realized what it had done, the puma fled in mortified surprise. Pumas are fond of porcupine meat, a taste that can be fatal if quills stuck in their face and paws prevent further hunting. Big cats seem to have no hesitation in eating little cats. Pumas have been known to eat both the bobcat and an occasional stray house cat. Although pumas are shy and nervous, they can be tamed if they are caught young. There is a story that the actor, Edmund Kean, who was notably flamboyant even for an actor, kept a tame puma that followed him about like a dog. The story should be taken as more typical of an actor than of a puma.

Midway between the big cats and the small are the lynxes. Some zoologists consider them a separate genus while others lump them with small cats in genus *Felis*. Lynxes come in many forms and are found in both the Old World and the New. They are long-legged cats with tufted ears and most have a stumpy tail, hence the popular term bobcat, usually applied to the American *Lynx rufus*. In the Old World, the caracal, sometimes called the Persian lynx, is a beautiful red-brown cat a bit bigger than a fox. It is easily tamed and, in India, trained to catch small deer and birds. In South Africa the Zulus make an ointment of its fat and an elegant cloak of its hide. Both are considered good for warding off rheumatism. Likewise in America, the fur of the bobcat and more often the Canada lynx is used for ladies' jackets and collars. They are worn even by ladies who are not threatened by rheumatism and are probably just as effective here as in Africa.

The bobcat is smaller than the Canada lynx and once ranged throughout the United States. It is a spotted cat whose buff-and-black or buff-and-gray coat is very much like that of a domestic tiger cat. In size bobcats vary from around twenty pounds to over fifty. Bobcats may still be found in the United States wherever there is wild country and small game, despite the efforts of farmers and stockmen bent on their extermination. The bobcat is amazingly strong.

It can bring down a two-hundred-pound buck, but it scorns nothing that flies, crawls or wiggles. Rodents are its staple, but grasshoppers, rattlesnakes, bats, crayfish and even skunks have been found inside bobcats.

When a bobcat is hunted with hounds it uses all the tricks of the fox, including running in circles. A mother with young will send the kittens up separate trees. A hunter in New Mexico had a rare opportunity to watch one wily old tom use a quite complex device. The huntsman, on horseback, saw the cat run up a tree while the hounds were still out of sight. Instead of staying there the cat ran down again, ran back over its own trail for fifty yards or so, and then made a mighty leap over a ridge. The hounds followed the stronger scent to the tree and sat there yelping while the bobcat made a clean getaway.

Taming a bobcat is almost impossible unless one starts with an infant that can be mothered by a suckling house cat. A few people have succeeded in raising bobcats and describe them as being very like a rougher, tougher, more active and possibly smarter house cat. A Texas bobcat that was the pet of an oil camp loved to ride in cars, drink beer from a saucer and wipe up the floor with passing dogs. An article in *Nature Magazine* described a pet bobcat that would roll over when its owner cried "dead cat" and played a fair game of hide-and-seek. It was also more restless, alert and curious than a house cat. Still another pet bobcat was inclined to pounce upon and eat passing house cats. The voice of the bobcat in captivity is just like that of the house cat. It purrs, mews and chirps just as eloquently, but its scream is hair-raising—a small version of the panther's, that literally carries for a mile.

South America is the home of dozens of small cats, ranging from the pampas cat and the wood cat of Argentina to the ocelot, jaguarondi and margay, which sometimes come as far north as the southwestern United States. Of these, the ocelot and the margay, which is smaller but very similar, not infrequently turn up as pets in the United States. They are both lovely to look at: black spotted cats whose ground color varies from chestnut to pale gold. Either can be bought on order from Trefflich's, a wild animal dealer in New York City, for around a hundred dollars, if the buyer insists. Trefflich's is reluctant to sell them as house pets and discourages customers with the warning that the cats may be dangerous when they grow up. Having long been tempted by the idea of a pet ocelot, I was grateful to find that a booklet about them had been written by Mrs. Catherine Phelan Cisin of Amagansett, founder of the Long Island Ocelot Club. Mrs. Cisin's booklet is frank and, to me, discouraging. She begins by saying that the ocelot and margay kittens for sale here have been trapped wild in the jungle and usually have endured a miserable and traumatic captivity before arriving at a pet store. They are apt to be undernourished, loaded with parasites and badly scared. They are so fragile, physically and emotionally, that they must be handled with great care, patience and veterinary skill. Even a shadow startles them. With luck the kitten does indeed become tame and behaves very much like a house cat, wrapping itself around its owner's legs, purring and meowing like a hoarse Siamese. At two years the cat is mature and, though still affectionate, has become twenty or thirty pounds of black and gold dynamite.

The ocelot is incredibly strong, fast and rough. It can leap eight feet straight up. Its sense of smell is extremely keen. It will, Mrs. Cisin says, choose the book or garment most recently touched by its owner as a plaything to tear up. Disengaging the cat from such a plaything is apparently no cinch, and success depends on the owner's skill in finding a diversion. The ocelot is naturally nocturnal. It loves night prowling. It is one of the cats that likes water and enjoys playing in the bathtub. It is willing to walk on a leash. It will come when called just as a house cat will, or, in other words, if it wants to. A tame ocelot soon learns to turn a doorknob with its teeth. It will use a cat pan, but the pan must have high sides since both male and female are inclined to spray standing up. Several owners have tried to breed ocelots without success. In captivity they often seem to be sterile. Futhermore, Mrs. Cisin warns, the mating of ocelots is a wild affair during which the fur flies. The cats are apt to hurt each other and more particularly any person who tries to interfere.

In Africa, Europe and Asia are found small cats even more various in type than in the western hemisphere. One of the most exotic and beautiful is Pallas' cat *(Felis manul)*, of Tibet, Siberia and Mongolia. It looks so much like a domestic longhair, having a long fluffy coat and broad head, that for a time it was believed to be the ancestral type, but this is no longer thought likely. It is generally a black and gray striped cat, but some of the hairs are tipped, giving a silvery wash effect.

Pallas' cat is one of the felines whose pupils remain round instead of narrowing to a slit in dim light. For all its beauty this cat seems rather formidable. At least the one I saw in a zoo gave me the most withering glare I've ever received from a cat.

Another baleful cat is the European wildcat, *Felis sylvestris,* and this is odd because it not only looks much like a big domestic tiger cat, but is suspected of having contributed to its ancestry. However that may be, I can find no record of successful taming of a European wildcat. Kittens raised in zoos have lost their friendliness as they grew up.

Wildcats were once plentiful all over Europe and the British Isles (though there were none in Ireland), but they now remain only in isolated places, out of reach of the ever-avenging farmer and husbandman. One such place is the wild west coast of Scotland where the cats have learned to subsist in great part on fish scooped out of the sea.

Africa and Asia have so many little cats that they are enumerated only in the most complete scientific works on the cat family. A number of north African species are popularly lumped together as Caffir cat or Egyptian cat, and it is among these that zoologists seek the progenitors of the domestic cat.

Chapter X

Cats of Many Colors

A survey of the family of cats makes it clear that the domestic cat's kinship with the wild is a close one, but it is not at all clear just what the relationship is. At some time, long ago, some sort of wildcat made the leap from jungle to hearth and that is about all that has ever been settled. Just which cat—or amalgamation of cats—gave rise to the domestics now populating the world is a matter of considerable puzzlement to those scientists who concern themselves with it. There are a good many small, wild species that resemble the domestic cat closely enough to be its first cousins, but none is identical with the domestic cat. After centuries of civilized life, the house cat has become a distinct species and within the species there are various types which compound the problem of identifying the ancestral stock.

Histories of the domestic cat usually begin with Egypt because there are comparatively complete records of domestic cats in Egypt, while evidence on domestic cats in other early cultures is extremely sketchy. Domestic cats are mentioned in both Chinese and Sanskrit writings of several thousand years ago, but there is no reason to suppose that these were the same kind of cats kept by the Egyptians. A modern domestic cat common in India is a small, spotted cat quite like a wild species named *Felis ornata* or Indian desert cat, that has a sandy yellow coat and lines of spots along the body. In fact the domestic and the wild are said to interbreed quite freely. Likewise in Europe the domestic cat can breed with its wild cousins of the continent.

This tendency of cats to get together at the slightest opportunity provides a further complication. Species, in its exact meaning, is a term to describe a kind of animal that generally does not breed with any other kind of animal. Or to put it another way around, other animals with which it can breed and produce young with the same characteristics are considered to be, by definition, within its species. When cross-matings do occur, as in horse and donkey, the result is usually sterile, as is the mule. With characteristic heedlessness cats don't pay much attention to this definition of species. The European wildcat *(Felis sylvestris)* and the domestic cat are certainly different species but yet, as has just been noted, they are suspected of consorting. Gavin Maxwell in *Ring of Bright Water* says that the "tawny, lynx-like feral wildcats in Scotland bear as much relation to the domestic cat as the wolf to the terrier. They are reportedly untameable, but the males sometimes mate domestic females. The offspring rarely survive, either because the sire returns to kill the kittens or because humans kill them. The wild strain is dominant, showing itself in lynx-like appearance and feral instinct. Halfbreeds usually take to the wild life."

A recent report in the *Journal of Mammology* describes the "presumed" mating of a male North American *Lynx rufus* with a domestic female in Utah. Of the five resulting kittens, three looked like lynxes and two like their domestic mother. They grew no bigger than large house cats, but all of them were very wild.

Some years ago the zoo in New York's Central Park was the proud possessor of an ambiguous looking beast produced in Germany by mating a male tiger and a lioness. It was called, naturally, a tiglon. I do not know if it was sterile, but its expression was sad and uncertain. The offspring of male lion and tigress is a liger and I believe that this, too, has occurred under artificial conditions.

However, even the most promiscuous cat cannot mate with a rabbit, a woodchuck, a skunk, or anything else that is not a cat, although folklore has long held that such freaks exist. Every now and then a "rabbitcat," "catchuck," "skunk-puss," "raccoon cat," or some such improbable beast is exhibited at a rural fair, or its photograph may show up in a local newspaper. Sometimes the owner will insist he saw its feline mother dallying in the twilight with the supposed father. This is an injustice to the fair name of the female cat who couldn't do such a thing if she wanted to. The strange-looking cats that show up from time to time are deformed or are mutations such as can occur in any species. The commonest mutation is one that gives the beast a rabbity look; buck rabbits are most often and improperly blamed for the sad result.

To get back to the early cat of Egypt, it is clear that the Egyptians had domestic cats because the tombs abound in pictures, statues and mummified bodies of cats. (Sometimes mummy cats were provided with mummy mice). The cat's importance in Egypt was twofold. Storage of grain was the keystone of the Egyptian economy and cats did a vital job in rodent control. Secondly, the cat became identified with the powerful moon goddess, one of whose names was Pasht, an identification that clings to the cat to this day in the word puss. (Another Egyptian word for cat was simply *Maou*.) Pasht was represented as a woman with the head of a cat. She symbolized the moon holding the light of the sun during the hours of darkness as the cat's eyes seem to. During an eclipse she fought the serpent of darkness which sought to consume the sun. Pasht was also the goddess of the chase and of love, two activities for which the cat is notable. In yet another version of moon mysticism, the cat is poetically represented as devouring the gray mice of twilight.

The religious symbolism of the cat accounts for the mummified bodies that have been found and for the peculiar rites and laws with which Egyptians surrounded cats. It was forbidden either to kill or to export a cat. Upon the death of a cat, its owners performed rites of formal mourning which required that they shave off their eyebrows and provide a ceremonious funeral.

(In this connection one might note that there are three pet cemeteries adjacent to New York City in which a cat funeral costs about $60. The cost of a cat funeral in ancient Egypt has not been computed, but one may safely guess that it was far less.)

In the last century, as the tombs were opened and Egyptian cemeteries excavated, mummified cats were found literally by the ton. They were a drug on the market. Shiploads of mummy cats were sent to England and auctioned off to be used as fertilizer. One auctioneer used an embalmed cat as a hammer. Now that mummies have become scarce, scientists regret this profligacy. Fortunately, enough specimens were saved to make it possible to identify the species. In 1907 a British expedition sent the British Museum a shipment of skulls from Gizeh, dating from 600 B.C. to 200 B.C., and consisting of a hundred and ninety-two cats, seven mongooses, three dogs and a fox. The box was put away and forgotten for some years, but was finally exhumed from the basement and examined. A British scientist, Dr. T. C. S. Morrison-Scot, has written that in his opinion the skulls were were of two races of cats, one resembling *Felis chaus* and the other *Felis lybica*. Both are small, wild species that survive in North Africa today.

After the Egyptian period, the story of the domestic cat once more becomes extremely misty. Despite the ban on its export, it is likely that the Egyptian cat traveled a good deal and, wherever it goes, the cat is a good mixer. The Romans kept cats, not necessarily pure Egyptian cats, and brought them to the British Isles, where, as Vesey-Fitzgerald puts it, they would have found plenty of wildcats anxious to make them feel at home. There are many mentions of cats in the medieval writings of Europe and Great Britain, but unfortunately the writers neglected to describe the lineage of the cats in question; to them a cat was obviously a cat, nothing more.

And this, too, is just about what we must content ourselves with today. A great many writers say categorically that all domestic cats are descended from the Egyptian cat. A categorical statement is more gratifying than an ambiguous one and it would be pleasant if this could be accepted as the whole story. What is much more likely is that domestic cats are a blend of many strains and that the mixture differs in different parts of the world. Furthermore, since cats have always been welcome on ships, these strains may now appear far, far from home. Such an answer is, of course, much too vague to be satisfying to the scientist and, since work is still being done on feline classification, there may someday be a more specific answer.

Cats are as stubborn genetically as they are temperamentally. Not only have they changed very little since they first appeared on earth, but they have refused to change in accordance with the wishes of people who breed them. Dogs have been more obliging. Starting from a few basic types, selective breeding has produced the most extraordinary variations. The exhibits at a dog show look more like the contents of Noah's ark than the members of one family. A cat show displays just one beast: the cat. There are several reasons for the difference. Dogs have been bred selectively for a much longer time than have cats and for more varied purposes; herding, sledge-drawing, and hunting in various styles are just a few of them. The uses of the cat are simpler. It is either ornamental or it is a mouse-catcher. When it comes to mousing, any size, shape or color of cat is as good as another. Breeding for ornamental purposes is a pastime that is rather rare and special. There has been, therefore, considerably less incentive to try to change the physique of the cat.

And here, once again, the cat's willfulness plays a part. Arranging a desired match for a dog is a relatively simple matter; to thwart a cat bent on misalliance is notoriously difficult. Usually only determined souls are willing to face the frustrations involved.

These considerations all bear on why there has been so little selective cat breeding, but the central factor is still the nature of cat genetics, the stubbornness of the basic type which resists attempts to change it by artificial selection. Unusual traits in cats have a tendency to disappear within a generation or two. Odd characteristics, a peculiar marking or color, are quickly swamped by just plain, ordinary cat.

The most ordinary version of plain cat is a gray, buff and black cat with dark stripes on tail, forehead and legs, and with dark swirls or stripes on its flanks. Likely as not it will have white under its chin or perhaps all over its underside. This is the classic tabby cat. Tabby does not refer to the sex of the cat. It is a word that has been used for centuries to describe the markings of the domestic cat and comes from the Arabic word *attabi*, designating a kind of watered silk with a swirling or moiré pattern. The same colors, black, gray and buff (with or without white), also occur in a pattern that I have always thought of as tiger, but that seems to be more properly called striped tabby. The striped markings correspond quite closely to those of many wild species, but oddly there is nothing in the wild exactly like the swirls on a tabby. Consequently blotched tabby markings are thought to be the result of a mutation that occurred after cats became domesticated. If so, it is one of the few that has really flowered. Blotched tabbies are as frequent, if not more so, than tiger-striped tabbies. The two types, blotched and striped, never mix. A cat is either striped or blotched, never partly one and partly the other.

Every domestic cat, no matter what it looks like, has the basic tabby in its genetic background. It seems surprising that so many colors and patterns can have sprung from variations on the basic theme of black, buff and gray, but it is accounted for by mutations, or new combinations, in the genes that make up the tabby coloration.

Genes are the factors in egg and sperm that enable traits to flow from one generation to the next. Groups of genes carried by chromosomes are the blueprints from which a new individual is fashioned. Each parent contributes one half of the genetic material and the halves fuse when egg and sperm unite. The germ plasm contributed by a parent is not necessarily a blueprint for an individual identical to the parent; it can contain genes derived from many ancestors who perhaps had differing traits. And since two parents contribute such material which may combine in numerous ways, the resulting individual is made from a slightly different mold than either parent. Genes not only control such gross qualities as size, shape and skeletal structure but determine the very last detail of the new individual down to the length of a hair or the placement of an eyelash.

In general, individuals within a species are pretty much alike, and produce offspring like themselves generation after generation. But from time to time a sudden variation occurs; the germ plasm within an individual egg or sperm suddenly takes on a new character, causing a change in one or more traits. This new gene takes the place of the old and is in turn transmitted down through successive generations.

The factor that makes a cat a tabby, or a cat of any other color, is not just one gene; it is a rather complex package of genes that interact and modify each other. There can be a mutation in just one or in several of these genes. Let's say that the tabby color package contains a dozen genes and that in each individual there may be a slight variation in one or more of the genes. With each parent contributing a package of a dozen variables, the number of possible combinations of the two becomes astronomical. That is why, if one got down to counting the hair on cats and classifying each hair, one would find that there are as many slightly different individuals as there are stars in the sky.

The tabby pattern of a cat is not a simple matter of dark hairs in one place and light in another. Each tabby hair is banded with buff, gray and black. Some of the hairs are banded in one pattern and some in another. This arrangement is known as the agouti pattern in honor of a South American rodent whose coat exemplifies it, though it occurs in a great many mammals.

The agouti factor provides plenty of scope for alteration. Any change in the way the hairs are banded will make a cat of a different color. Beyond that, the package of color genes contains factors that modify color, strengthening it or diluting it, while still other sets determine overall pattern—whether the coat will be solid color or have spots, stripes and blotches in particular places.

To say that all the possible varieties of color are due to mutation is not to imply that a mutation has occurred each time a kitten is born that differs from its parents. More likely it occurred way back in the kitten's ancestral line. Sometimes, for instance, a black kitten is a throwback, the result of a mutation that may have occurred long before and been carried through many generations of tabbies, but this mutant black gene did not produce any black kittens until a mating occurred in which both parents carried in it their germ plasm. This capacity of a gene to remain present but latent is due to the rules of dominance and recessiveness; the so-called Mendelian laws of heredity.

Most of us remember—though perhaps hazily, since the subject quickly becomes quite confusing—that when a trait has two contrasting forms, one is likely to conceal the other. Short hair and long hair in cats are contrasting forms of the same trait. Short hair dominates long hair. A pure short-haired cat mated to a pure long-haired cat produces short-haired kittens. Of this litter of short-haired kittens, some carry a recessive or hidden gene for long hair and some don't. You can't tell which is which by looking at them. But the mating of two short-haired cats with hidden genes for long hair will produce long-haired kittens in a ratio of one out of four.

It is by now obvious that the genetics of cats defy any attempt to put them in a nutshell, but since we've come this far it may be worthwhile to take a look at the principal color factors responsible for the myriad kinds of cats.

Tabby: This is a combination of the agouti factor with an independent striping factor. Tabby is dominant.

Non-agouti: This gene, the opposite of agouti, prevents the banding of the hairs so that they become all black. The non-agouti black hairs merge with the black hairs of the tabby stripes so that the coat is black all over. Sometimes, though, the stripes contrast enough to show a ghost pattern of tabby. Non-agouti is recessive.

Brown: Brown cats can be produced by several combinations of genes. In addition there is believed to be a distinct gene for brown. It is a recessive mutation and rather rare.

Color suppression genes: Color suppression is the result of a series of genes that reduce the amount of pigmentation. These genes occur in a graduated series. The mildest form merely modifies black to brown, while in full strength there is albinism, or no pigment at all. (The albino has pink eyes because absence of pigment in the iris allows the red of the blood vessels to be seen). The series ranges from full color through silver, Burmese, Siamese to pure white. Color suppression affects yellow pigment more strongly than black, which accounts for the shadings of animals in this series. (Removal of yellow produces silver; removal of yellow and some black produces brown, etc.)

Maltese dilution: This is a recessive factor that dilutes black to gray and yellow to cream. Diluted blacks are now termed blues, although they still look gray to me. Dilution affects the stripes as well as the ground color. They may be so diluted that the coat appears solid, or diluted to a darker shade of the ground color, producing a blue or yellow tabby.

Dominant black: This is believed to be a mutation of the factor governing the extension of black, as in the points of the Siamese.

Yellow: A gene that modifies black pigment produces yellow. It may be reinforced, turning the coat to orange or red, or it may be diluted to cream color. It is a curious gene. Because it is incompletely dominant, it may interact with tabby or black to produce tortoise-shell. The yellow gene is linked to the gene determining sex in such a way that tortoise-shells are almost always female. Male tortoise-shells do appear from time to time. They are usually sterile, but fertile males have occurred and thrown geneticists in to a quandary. Possible explanations for the anomaly fill volumes of scientific literature.

Piebald spotting: Patches of white are due to a factor that, like the albino, occurs in various intensities. The series begins with one white hair and ends (possibly) in white all over. The white patches follow a recognized pattern. The first touch of white appears on the chest. The next grade of spotting adds white to the feet. As the grades progress, they add white on the groin and belly, up the sides to encircle the neck, and finally along the back. Colored patches on the head, back and tail are the last to disappear.

Dominant white: This may be the product of the end of the spotting series, or it may be a separate gene. In either case these white cats are not albinos. They may be blue-eyed or yellow-eyed or have one blue and one yellow eye. Hereditary deafness is usually, though not always, associated with blue-eyed white cats.

Of course there is more to a cat than its color. All its other physical traits are likewise controlled by genes and in these, too, there are some interesting variations.

The most obvious is long hair versus short hair. Long hair

usually behaves as recessive. There is no proof that it originated in Turkey—whence came the now discarded term
Angora—or in Persia, which gave us the still-current term
Persian for a long-haired cat. Long-haired cats seem to have
appeared in Europe in the late fifteen hundreds. The long
hair of the domestic breed is not like the long hair of any of
the wild species. Peter Simon Pallas, a German naturalist,
who traveled in Russia in the late seventeen hundreds, thought
he had discovered the origin of domestic long-hairs when he
came across *Felis manul* (Pallas' cat), but this is now dis-
counted because the *manul* has a different skull structure
and a round eye pupil. There are several grades of hair
length. Semi-long hair is more frequent in females. Castra-
tion will increase the length of hair in a male. Long hair can
be combined with any of the color types of short-haired
cats.

An odd mutation of the genes governing the type of hairs
in the coat can produce a cat with a short, curly coat and
curly whiskers, known as a rex coat. The normal fur of cats
is composed of four distinct types of hairs of different lengths
and thickness which overlap to make up the undercoat and
the outer coat. In the rex cat it seems that all or most of the
hairs of types one, two and three are missing, leaving only
the fourth type, the down hairs of the undercoat. The down
hairs are crimped and in the rex cat they are even shorter
than normal. The result is a very short, very soft, wavy coat.
The rex mutation is both rare and recessive so that to preserve it rex cats must be inbred.

Still another mutation causes the occasional birth of an
unfortunate cat suffering from what is scientifically referred
to as hypotrichosis. In other words, the poor beast is naked
as a jay bird. They are rare and, except in warm climates,
likely to freeze to death before they can perpetuate the gene.

There are references, fairly vague and elusive, suggesting that naked cats were once known as a breed in Mexico, but as far as I can find, no one has seen such a cat lately.

Extra toes, or mitten-feet, in cats are due to a mutation that is dominant and has become extremely widespread. It can vary from an enlargement of one toe to the addition of two new toes. It can affect all four feet or just the front feet. The hind feet never have mittens unless the front feet have them.

Dwarf cats are another genetic possibility about which not much is known. As a rule, undersized cats are the result of malnutrition or disease, but a family of miniatures producing miniature kittens was recorded in England a few years ago. Without protection such a mutation would disappear quite quickly. When cats are on their own, it is the biggest, toughest tomcats that sire the most kittens. This factor of selection has also been suggested as an explanation for the spread of certain colors through a population of cats. If color is by any chance linked to an aggressive temperament, it would be likely to drive out the colors carried by meeker toms.

Mutations not infrequently affect the tail of the cat. Siamese are apt to have a kink in the tail, and short or bent tails are quite common in the plain cats of Eastern Asia. Tails may be bobbed or be missing entirely. The mutant gene for taillessness appears to be dominant. Its spread is perhaps checked by a related factor that causes stillborn or weak kittens. Tailless cats are also called Manx cats, since there was at one time a legend that they originated on the Isle of Man. Cat fanciers have conferred on tailless cats the title of breed. They come in all colors.

Another oddity deliberately perpetuated by breeders is a long-haired cat with a peke face. This is just what it sounds like; a change in the bone structure of the face gives the cat a wrinkled muzzle, indented nose and pop eyes.

Common tabby cats most often have pale yellow or gray-green eyes, but sometimes the eyes are orange, pure green or blue. In purebred cats deep orange or copper-colored eyes have been selected as desirable for most of the breeds other than Siamese. There have been almost no scientific studies of the genetics of eye-color in cats, but it is obvious that in some cases eye-color and coat-color are linked. The albino factors seem to prevent full pigmentation and result in the green to sapphire eyes of cats in the silver to white series.

Finally, we come to the shape of the cat. Two distinct genetic types exist, the stocky and the rangy. The British like stocky cats, and their purebred cats have been selected accordingly. The ideal British cat has a powerful body (cobby is the British word), a short, thick tail, a broad head and slightly rounded ears. The common American cat is generally lighter and longer, more willowy and with more aquiline features; the physique of Abraham Lincoln compared to that of Winston Churchill is an analogy that springs to mind. The British term cats of rangy build the foreign variety. In addition, the British feel that their cat is distinctly British in personality—bluff and hearty, fond of outdoor sports, loyal, tolerant and with a sense of fair play. At least this is the description given in one of the better British cat books and I found that it instantly aroused my chauvinism, particularly as I can't ascribe all these virtues to any of the American cats I've owned. Minnie is moderately loyal and very fond of the outdoors. But she is certainly intolerant, one might almost say narrow-minded. She loves games, but her sense of fair play is nil. She consistently cheats at cards.

Chapter XI

The Fashionable Cat

Natural or randomly created cats come off the assembly line as assorted as the colors in a package of Necco wafers. Purebred cats are a different kettle of fish. They are cats that have been bred selectively in order to combine certain traits: length of coat, color, markings, eye color and conformation, according to specified rules. About forty such combinations of traits are now considered to be breeds.

To the uninitiated, a number of these breeds look very much like plain cat and in truth they are. This doesn't mean that any old cat can wander into the cat show at Madison Square Garden and walk off with a ribbon, but on the other hand there are as many undiscovered champion-type cats wasting their time in barns and alleys as there are farmers' daughters pretty enough to go on the stage.

The difference between purebred and plebeian is often rather technical. A handsome, pure-black, short-haired cat with coppery eyes may be cat show material while its twin brother with green eyes is nothing but an alley cat. Some of the fanciest breeds of cats differ from the common tabby by no more than a single mutant gene. Since most of these mutant genes are recessive, the prized characteristics will vanish in the course of one or two generations of mating with common cats. Breeds of cats are, therefore, rather ephemeral things. On the other hand, the mutant gene, though gone, is not forgotten. It remains hidden in some of the plain cats descended from the flossy ancestor and when chance brings about the right combination it will pop up again.

The result is that while professional breeders often get unwelcome surprises in purebred litters, the owner of a homely no-account tabby may be charmed to find that it has given birth to a highly aristocratic kitten.

The qualities that go to make up aristocracy in a cat are defined by the governing bodies of the cat clubs. The idea of purebred cats and competition at cat shows originated in England in the eighteen seventies. British catdom is ruled by the Governing Council of the Cat Fancy, whence the pleasant term The Fancy to describe a circle of cat-fanciers. In America things have been far less stable in the cat world and no single organization governs all the cat clubs. Associations of cat clubs have formed, split and formed new groups at such a rate that only the most dedicated historians are able to keep track. At present the Cat Fanciers' Association, with a membership of a hundred and nineteen clubs in the United States and Canada, is the largest, but the Cat

Fanciers Federation and the American Cat Association are also large and active organizations.

The world of the fashionable cat strikes outsiders as being pretty special. Some say that the best way for an amateur to tell if a cat is aristocratic or plain is to observe its owner closely. If the owner throws around terms such as queen (meaning female cat), in kitten (meaning pregnant), polishes the cat with a piece of chamois as though it were family silver, or remarks deprecatingly that its ears are too big or its nose leather lacks the proper shade of pink, it is likely that the cat is a purebred. Not everyone, however, may have this opportunity. For the benefit of those who would, nevertheless, like to be informed, here is a run-down of the main breeds.

Purebred cats are divided into two classes, long-haired and short-haired. With a few exceptions long-haired and short-haired cats come in the same colors and patterns. A long-haired cat is basically no more than a short-haired cat in which the gene for long hair has replaced the ordinary gene for short hair. Take a purebred tabby cat, mate it with a long-haired cat of any color, and the offspring are plain tabby cats because long hair is recessive, while short hair and tabby markings are dominant. But if you then inbreed two of the tabbies from this litter, you may get a long-haired tabby, which is a recognized breed eligible for showing. In any single instance luck plays a part because you must somehow divine which of your plain, look-alike tabbies harbor the latent gene for long hair. Breeding cats thus has some of the thrills of the shell game.

Theoretically long-hairs and short-hairs may differ in only one gene, but show specifications call for slightly different conformation in the two types and they have been selectively bred accordingly. The long-hair is required to have a stocky build with short, solid legs, deep chest and a massive round head. It should carry its tail straight and low (but not dragging), and have large, round, wide-set eyes giving a "sweet expression to the face." The last is quoted from the 1960 rules of the Cat Fanciers Federation which go on to say: "It is particularly desirable to eliminate rangy, flat-sided, narrow-chested, long, spindle-legged, long-tailed cats, with long noses, large ears pointed and upright, eyes set bias and close together, receding chins, light bone and a general 'foxy' face." (To me not all these traits seem as odious as they apparently are to the Cat Fanciers Federation. I rather like big-eared, slanty-eyed, rangy cats, but this will get me nowhere with the authorities. Furthermore, I have never in my life seen an animal combining such a formidable list of undesirable qualities, but there must have been such cats or the Cat Fanciers wouldn't be trying to eliminate them. (Could it be that word of their social standing somehow reached them and they all committed suicide in shame?) Finally, the coat of the long-haired cat should be fine, soft, glossy, full of life, and should stand off from the body. The ruff should be "immense" and continue in a deep frill between the front legs. Long, curved ear tufts and long toe tufts are also desirable.

Short-haired cats are not expected to be as massive as long-haired cats, but they should be sturdy, athletic types. Show standards describe the short-haired domestic as "well-knit and powerful with a broad chest, strong legs, small and neat feet, small, rounded ears, and a broad head with a short nose." A short tail is preferable to a long tail and it should be carried level. Receding chins, rangy legs and Roman noses are frowned upon. Siamese cats, Russian Blues, Burmese and Abyssinian cats are allowed to have lighter bones, longer tails and more wedge-shaped faces than the other short-haired breeds.

The most generally recognized breeds of cats are listed below:

Black with orange eyes

Blue with orange eyes

White with orange eyes or blue eyes

Red with orange eyes

Cream with orange eyes

Tortoise-shell or Calico with orange eyes

Blue Cream with orange eyes

Tabbies, in Silver with green, brown, blue or red eyes, or Cameo with orange eyes.

Color Point or Himalayan with blue eyes

Silvers: Chinchilla and Shaded Silver with green eyes, Smoke with orange eyes

Cameo: Shell Cameo, Shaded Cameo or Smoke Cameo with orange eyes.

Abyssinian

Burmese

Siamese

Russian Blue

Manx

Here in general are the genetics and show points of pure-bred cats.

Black: Black cats are tabby cats in which the non-agouti gene in both parents has wiped out the ticking of the hairs, making them all black. The tabby stripes are still present, but since they are also black they no longer show, although kittens are apt to show a ghost pattern of stripes. Common black cats are quite frequent, but are very likely to have a bit of white on the chest. They may have green or yellow eyes. The perfect black show cat must not have a single white hair, and fashion further decrees orange or copper eyes. (In fact dark yellow eyes are demanded in purebred cats of all colors or mixtures of color with the exception of the Silvers,

Siamese, White and Russian Blue.) Coal-black cats with orange eyes are hard to breed. If you see one lounging outside your neighborhood delicatessen, grab it and rush it off to the nearest cat show.

Blue: Blue cats are non-agouti blacks with a gene for dilution added. The dilution gene is recessive, so blue cats can crop up quite unexpectedly in apparently undistinguished families. Blues naturally occur in various shades from slate to very pale. In show cats the lighter shades are preferred. Tabby markings are quite apt to show through, so if you buy an expensive blue cat, watch out for rings on its tail. Long-haired blues are highly thought of by The Fancy, but recently a type of short-haired blue known as Russian Blue has been coming up fast on the outside, perhaps because of intense promotion and publicity efforts by a New York cattery which boasts of having imported one from the Soviet Union and sold it for $1000 to an unnamed purchaser. The seller needn't have bothered sending to Russia, since blue cats, exactly like Russian Blues, have been known in Britain and America for as long as anyone has been keeping track of cats, and good ones are also bred in Denmark.

There is, of course, the usual complement of legends about the origin of Russian Blues. In one account they came from the city of Archangel, but in the more usual account they came straight from the Imperial Palace. (Fancy mutations occur no more frequently in palaces than anywhere else and are not the result of any sort of radiation from the aristocratic human penetrating the lowly house cat and causing it to have aristocratic kittens. However palace walls could indeed confine a population of cats so that mutations would not be lost through breeding with common cats.) Disinterested authorities—*i.e.*, not breeders—consider Russian Blues simply the familiar mutation from black to blue coupled with a certain bone structure and eye color. Vesey-Fitzgerald reports finding a real beauty of a Russian Blue gracing a humble English farm house. It was the daughter of a tortoise-shell and from time to time gave birth to splendid Russian Blue kittens. To be considered Russian, a blue should be tall and slender, with a short, fine, lustrous coat, and have vivid green eyes. It is indeed a lovely type of cat.

White: Pure white cats with pigmented eyes possess a dominant gene for whiteness that is believed to be quite distinct from the albino gene of white cats with pink eyes. White is dominant over all other colors and yet, curiously, pure white cats are not very frequent. Possibly this gene is linked with other factors that reduce the percentage of live kittens. White cats come with blue eyes, yellow eyes or pale green eyes. Sometimes one eye is green and the other yellow or blue. Blue-eyed white cats, it is well known, are very apt to be deaf. It is interesting that a cat with one blue eye may be deaf only in the ear nearest to the blue eye. Pure white cats are a show breed. Either blue or orange eyes are acceptable, but not green.

Red: Red cats are the product of the peculiar yellow gene which modifies black and eliminates ticking. Most frequently a yellow cat is the color of marmalade, but when other quite mysterious factors came into play, rufinism or redness is produced. Yellow cats have no social status, but red cats do. Dark red cats are scarce and hard to breed. They are more apt to be red tabby than solid red. Solid red long-hairs have been bred from mixing blue cats, cream cats and red tabby cats.

Cream: Here we have the yellow gene again, more prized by breeders when it is in a mixture than when it appears alone. In cream cats the yellow is diluted by the same gene that dilutes black to blue. In other words, blue cat plus yellow cat equals cream cat. To meet show standards, the cream color cannot show tabby stripes or be too hot—that is, a strong, or orangey, yellow.

Tortoise-shell and *Calico:* The pied coat of the tortoise-shell can come in several color combinations and literally endless arrangements. Basically the tortoise-shell is a mixture of yellow and black. The colors may be intermingled in a brindled, salt-and-pepper style, or segregated in patches. The yellow patches may be creamy or dark red or both. Tabby stripes may show here and there. The yellow gene is incompletely recessive and seems to assert itself in one place on the cat but not in another. The behavior of the yellow gene could be described, unscientifically, as notional. Tortoise-shells appear quite frequently, but it is almost impossible to breed a particular pattern to order. Show standards call for black, orange and cream, in patches—not brindled—and the splashiest-looking cats are preferred. The addition of white patches to tortoise-shell is called Calico.

Blue Cream: A blue cream is a tortoise-shell with a gene for dilution softening the black and yellow. In Great Britain a brindled pattern is preferred, but United States standards call for patches as in the tortoise-shell. Just as in tortoise-shells, blue creams are almost always female.

Tabby: The tabby pattern of black stripes on a light ground is the result of two factors: the agouti factor which bands the hairs of the ground color, and the striping factor which lays the dark stripes over it. There are several variations in the pattern of stripes. Blotched stripes may be wide or narrow. Tiger stripes may be dark and clear, or very narrow and close together. They may break up into spots or even disappear entirely. The last two possibilities—the spotted tabby and the all-gray tabby (not to be confused with a blue cat)—occur naturally but they are very rare. So far as I'm aware, no one has tried to breed them.

The persistence of the ancestral tabby causes breeders much pain. Genetically this is *the* breed of cat, but it is only allowed in the show ring in fancy colors. Silver Tabby (black stripes on silver ground), Red Tabby (red with darker red stripes), Blue Tabby (ivory and pale blue ground with dark blue stripes), Brown Tabby (black stripes on chestnut ground) and Cameo Tabby (cream ground color with red markings) are all highly prized breeds. On a purebred cat that isn't supposed to have tabby markings, the stripes are a badge of shame.

Although theoretically any color may be as easily bred in a short-haired as in a long-haired cat, or vice versa, there are a few breeds that come only in short hair or long hair.

Silver Cats: Chinchilla, Shaded Silver and Smoke are the names given to three breeds of long-haired cats that have been produced by adding the weakest albino gene to solid color cats, and they are very spectacular cats. The chinchilla has a white undercoat topped with a black-ticked overcoat which gives a silvery effect. The eyes are green. Shaded Silver is similar, but darker. A Smoke cat wears a black overcoat and pale gray underwear. The points are black, but the frill and ear tufts are silver. The eyes are copper.

Cameo: This is a recently developed breed of long-haired cats carrying both silver and yellow genes. They are generally beige with darker-tipped hairs. The Shell Cameo is almost white with very slight tipping. The Shaded Cameo is reddish shading to cream. The Smoke Cameo is a deep ruddy beige with a cream undercoat and cream shadings.

Color Point or Himalayan: This is an example of the transfer of coloring from a short-haired to a long-haired breed.

The color point has Siamese coloration on the typically stocky frame of the long-haired cat. Because of the difference in build between the Color Point and the Siamese, breeders emphatically deny that it is a long-haired Siamese.

Siamese: Siamese are, of course, short-haired only. They are an old and much loved breed. It has been estimated that eighty per cent of the purebred cats sold these days are Siamese. Need it be said that the story of how the original pair of sacred cats was stolen from a Buddhist temple is hard to verify? Or add that there are very few Siamese cats in Siam? Wherever they may have come from, Siamese cats have been known and bred selectively in the United States since the turn of the century. The British seem to have had them first. This long history of selective breeding of Siamese has produced cats that differ from common cats in several ways. The Siamese personality isn't easy to define to the satisfaction of all lovers of Siamese, except to say they seem to have more personality than other cats. They are highly independent and yet form deep attachments to people. They resist discipline in true cat fashion, and yet are slightly more amenable to instruction. They are both high-strung and highly communicative.

The body type preferred by breeders of Siamese is a willowy cat of medium size. Inbreeding tends to produce smaller animals and may account for Siamese being a bit smaller than the ordinary domestic cat. "Dainty, long and svelte" is the way the Cat Fanciers Federation describes the ideal Siamese. The head should be long and wedge-shaped, with a long, straight nose; large, pricked ears; slanted, almond-shaped eyes. The tail should be long and taper to a point, the feet small and oval.

Show standards don't mention the notable vocal talent that has somehow been bred into Siamese. Around the house they are inclined to "talk" loudly and insistently. Some people like this and others find it gets on their nerves.

Geneticists, who aren't much interested in stories of sacred temples unless they can be proved, think that the explanation for the Siamese can be found in the genes called the albino alleles. An allele is an opposite. The albino alleles inhibit the development of full color, and are thus the opposites of full color. At the top of the series, (*i.e.*, the weakest grade of albino), the gene converts the basic color to silver. The series proceeds, with more albinism, through Burmese (color converted to sable), Siamese (color converted to fawn), to albino which has no pigment at all. Albinos still carry their original color genes and color will reappear in their offspring whenever it is freed from the inhibiting effect of the albino gene. The albino gene also progressively changes the pigmentation of the eyes, from gray-blue in the silver to pure sapphire in the Siamese.

It takes more than the single mutation of albinism to change tabby to Siamese. There is also the non-agouti factor and probably the gene for dominant black which suppresses the tabby markings. The factors suppressing color work more effectively on some parts of the body than others. Thus, in the Siamese, there is more albinism in the body coloration while dark pigment develops on the extremities to produce the points.

It is interesting that temperature affects the formation of pigment. Lower temperature allows more pigment to form. This has been shown in an experiment in which a Siamese kept in a temperature under forty degrees gradually turned several shades darker. A patch of the dark fur was then shaved and the spot bandaged so that body heat kept the skin under the bandage at almost body temperature. When, six weeks later, the bandage was taken off, the new fur was a mingling of pure white hairs and brown-tipped hairs. Skin temperature, of course, is not uniform on the body of any animal. In humans, noses, fingers and toes feel the cold before the middle does. Likewise, the extremities of a cat are colder. It seems possible, then, that skin temperature influences the points on Siamese. It is also known that the thyroid gland has a further influence on Siamese coloration. A fawn Siamese darkens to chocolate if its thyroid is removed. Siamese kittens are white when they are born and the dark areas develop gradually. If kittens are stimulated by early handling they darken more quickly than kittens that are left alone.

The whole set of Siamese traits is recessive to full color so that usually half-breeds of Siamese and common cats produce very plain cats, but sometimes in a later generation there is an unusually happy combination that results in a highly distinguished-looking animal. It may be much admired at home, but in a cat show can compete only in the class tactfully termed Household Pet.

The traditional and most frequent color of a Siamese is fawn combined with seal points, but in recent years breeders have been fiddling around with the color genes and have come up with chocolate points, orange points, lilac points, blue points (not to be confused with oysters), and frost points, on backgrounds of varying paleness. Frost Point Siamese are almost white.

Burmese: Burmese are short-haired cats midway between domestic and Siamese in build. The coat is a solid sable brown with very slightly darker shading on the points. The eyes are yellow. They possess the albino factor in a grade midway between Silver and Siamese. Whether they have other genetic differences from the Siamese is not known, but they are certainly not as vocal.

Abyssinian: The Abyssinian is a light brown cat without markings but with intense ticking on the hairs in two or three bands of light and dark brown. The tip of the hair is the darkest. The eyes may be hazel, gold or green. The paw pads are black and the long, tapering tail is faintly marked with a black line along its length and has a black tip. Dark bars inside the legs and mackerel spots on the belly are accepted at shows, but not encouraged. The Abyssinian is a tall, slim cat with a rather small head, long neck and large ears. The usual legends surround its origin, including that of direct descent from the Egyptian temple cats, but again disinterested authorities are inclined to regard it as a breed manufactured in Britain from selected tabbies. These cats have been recognized as a breed almost as long as Siamese, but it can be disputed whether the earliest registered Abyssinians were really Abyssinian, which makes the exact date hard to determine.

Manx: Manx cats, although their chief characteristic—lack of a tail—might be thought of as a deformity, are nevertheless considered a breed and are eligible for showing. All colors and markings are allowed, but no trace of a tail.

While the breeds described above are those recognized by the majority of cat associations, the list cannot be considered the final word on breeds. The several associations by no means agree on all points. Then, too, new breeds are admitted to the cat Social Register from time to time. The British, for instance, have a short-haired breed called the Chestnut Brown that is the same shade as the dark points of a Siamese, but is evenly colored all over. They have been developed comparatively recently from black cats modified by crossing with Siamese. Their eyes are green. They have been known also as Havana Brown, not because they have anything to do with Cuba but after a fancy breed of rabbits known as Havanas.

There are few additional types of cats that are not, however, recognized breeds in the United States.

The Turkish are said to breed an Ankara cat that is all

white and has one green eye and one blue eye. Another Turkish variety, equally exotic, has a long-haired white coat, an auburn tail ringed in darker colors, and auburn stripes on the head.

A long-haired cat known in France as the Burman—or Sacred Cat of Burma, since this is yet another refugee from a temple—looks like an extraordinarily flashy, long-haired Siamese. The body coat is golden and fluffy, the tail, mask and ears are dark chocolate and the feet are white.

A Magpie cat is a black and white cat spotted in a piebald pattern like a Dutch-colored rabbit, and is regrettably so rare that it may be extinct.

The Maine coon cat is one that seems to have developed itself without human interference. It has very thick, semi-long hair, as any sensible cat in Maine would wish to have.

There has been a good deal of discussion among owners and partisans of this or that breed of cat comparing the personality traits of the various breeds. Some think that one breed is sweeter, smarter, lazier, a hunter and so on. My own feeling is that there is a wide difference in personality among individual cats, but that distribution of traits is impartial among the breeds, with the exception, perhaps, of the Siamese.

If you are going to buy a purebred cat, the choice of breed depends on the looks and type that appeal to you and the amount of money you wish to spend. Judging personality is an intuitive matter for which there are no reliable rules.

It is also hard to generalize about the price of a purebred cat. Much depends on how perfect a specimen it is by the standards of that breed. Generally speaking, Abyssinians, Burmese, Siamese and Russian Blues are the more expensive breeds. Long-haired kittens with some sort of lineage can be bought from $15 up. A hundred dollars should buy quite a fancy cat. The price needn't stop there by any means, though for me it certainly does.

Perhaps the only cat that could persuade me to spend more would be a short-haired, green-eyed little cat with a bright yellow coat, striped in coal black, and with a white belly; in other words a perfect, tiny tiger. Something put this romantic possibility into my head years ago when, at the age of about ten, I became a dedicated cat-keeper. Whenever our dear old brood cat was expecting kittens I dreamed that a kitten like this would be among the litter. It never was and I now suppose, mundanely, that the reason it can't be is because yellow and black interact differently in the domestic cat than they do in the tiger. Nonetheless I still sometimes look wistfully at Minnie—who has the stripes but not the yellow—and hope that on one of her midnight outings some wonderful encounter will occur—and that she will oblige me after all.

Chapter XII

Cats in Trouble

How are things going for cats today? For some, the lucky cats, it is a golden age. Wherever there is rich and rural country with farms and barns there are sleek and happy cats. These are working cats that may or may not have a close relationship with their landlords. In the meanwhile a different class of cat, the pet cat with no duties except to keep people company, is gaining greater favor. These days, more and more people not only love cats as pets, but value them, taking trouble over their care rather than simply having them around as loosely attached adjuncts to the household.

There are very few accurate figures on cat population, but there are indications of trends. The sale of purebred cats, for instance, is higher than ever before. So is the demand for veterinary service for cats. A few years ago there was practically no such thing as a cat specialist, and cats were treated, sometimes a bit grudgingly, as part of a veterinarian's general practice. In fact, except for breeders to whom a cat had cash value, it simply didn't occur to most people to take a cat to a veterinarian. If a cat was hurt or sick it either lived or died without expert assistance. We have now become more medically conscious on all fronts, and cats are included in the benefits. One of the results is that cats, like people, are enjoying a longer life span, and veterinarians are confronted with a new problem: feline geriatrics.

Another indicator of a trend in the lives of cats is the sale of commercial food. This has been climbing higher every year. In 1960 sixty million dollars worth of canned food was consumed by the nation's cats. An eight-ounce can of commercial food costs approximately ten cents so that six hundred million cans were eaten. Of course no one knows how many went into an individual cat, but it is nevertheless an indication that a large number of cats were well fed.

The relatively new business of providing accoutrements of various kinds for cats is also booming. In the old days cats came into the world equipped with all the material possessions they would ever need and no one racked his brains thinking up things to give the cat that had everything. If anyone had suggested to my grandfather that he could make his fortune providing scratching posts for cats, or by designing a better catnip mouse, he'd have laughed his head off. But times have changed, and catnip-mouse manufacturers are among the beneficiaries. Some cat accessories strike one as being things that even the most effete cat could get along

177

quite well without, but others, such as deodorizing litter, can be a great convenience.

Crowded quarters are the key to everything in the life of the modern cat, as much as in the life of the modern human. In one sense cats are profiting by the trend to urban and suburban living. In another they are suffering from it. The statistics provided by humane societies in the larger towns suggest that as people find housing more cramped they turn to the cat as a more practical pet than a dog.

A study by the Anti-Cruelty Society of Chicago showed that between 1950 and 1960 the city's dog population had shrunk considerably, while in the same period the ratio of cats vs. dogs adopted from their shelter changed significantly in favor of cats.

It would be nice if one could say that because of the rising popularity of cats their horizon as a species is rosier than ever before, but unfortunately there is more to the story than this.

Cats lucky enough to have owners are leading splendid lives, but the existence of the stray cat is more precarious each year. In New York City, for instance, where stray cats teem in uncounted thousands, conditions are becoming ever more inhospitable. Traditionally, the city's stray cats were more or less working cats that were encouraged to hang around warehouses, wharves and small markets. Now modern improvements are diminishing these opportunities one by one. Better rat-proofing and packaging are not only making things difficult for rats, but are putting dockside and warehouse cats out of work. The same thing is true of the small food stores that once supported the fattest, handsomest alley cats in town. There are fewer small stores now. Many of those that remain buy meat cut up and wrapped so there are no scraps to be thrown to the cat.

Finally, that proverbial last resort of the stray cat, the

sidewalk garbage can, is being replaced by chutes and incinerators, so that here, too, the pickings are getting poorer.

And yet, somehow, the stray cats of New York go on and struggle through enough of a lifetime to create all too many more homeless kittens. The American Society for the Prevention of Cruelty to Animals estimates that the life span of the average stray in New York City is about two years. The strays live in subways, backyards, cellars and crannies of all sorts. They call and wail in the backyards and creep along the gutters under the parked cars. They die of disease, food poisoning, starvation and exposure. These cats are wild and shy; one seldom sees them close at hand. One summer night not long ago, though, I happened to work late in a small ground-floor shop in midtown Manhattan. The back door into the alley was open and as darkness fell the yowling of the strays began. Then, cautiously, a few sneaked in to look around for bits of food. I threw them the remains of my supper and they furtively crept near. I reached for one, a half-grown kitten, and then drew back. This was the first cat I'd ever seen in my life that I didn't dare touch. It was covered with sores and filth, so starved that its head seemed huge and its flanks flat as paper. For the first time I really understood, emotionally as well as practically, why the ASPCA speaks of the kindness of destroying such luckless animals as these.

In the country things are somewhat better for homeless cats, but even so there is less and less room for them. Much as I love cats, I have sadly come to the conclusion that homeless cats should not be allowed to be.

The Humane Society of the United States estimates that fifty million kittens are born annually and points out that there are simply not enough families in the United States to absorb them. More than half of the annual crop of kittens must be destroyed sooner or later, and if it is later it means that even more cats must die the following year.

The destruction of cats is not a pleasant, an easy or an inexpensive matter. Already humane organizations and public pounds are spending fifty million dollars a year to destroy unwanted dogs and cats. The more efficient, *i.e.*, more painless, ways of killing are not always used in smaller communities. The decency with which animals are handled in public pounds varies tremendously from community to community. Like all public officers, pound keepers do the best they can under the circumstances and won't do better unless the public insists on it.

There are about five hundred humane societies in the United States—some large, some small—supported by private contributions and doing a job as necessary to a community as street sweeping. Where they don't do this job, each individual is all too often faced with the choice of becoming a one-man humane society or of turning away hungry or injured cats and dogs. Neither course is pleasant and a person in that position has a right to reflect indignantly that the problem has been dumped upon him through the carelessness of someone else—the person who left the animal to fend for itself.

Not all communities are covered either by a humane society or an efficient animal warden paid by town funds. Where a community has no adequate service, it is up to the people who care about animals to organize one themselves. It sounds like a big undertaking, but it isn't as difficult as one would think. Until a few years ago, the New England town in which I happen to live had no humane society. Its dog officer was a political appointee whose real job was garbage collection. If a householder complained about a stray dog or cat camping on the doorstep, the dog officer would promise to come and shoot it when he got the time. As the town became less rural and more suburban, with more and more summer visitors arriving to nurture summer kittens and toss them out in the autumn, the problem began to get on people's nerves. Finally a few citizens got together, raised some funds, and started an animal shelter that is now doing an indispensable job. It not only does away with unwanted animals in a humane fashion, but provides first aid, finds homes for puppies and kittens, and gets lost animals back home. Anyone who feels stirred to follow this example might begin by getting in touch with whatever organization covers the nearest big city. Advice, encouragement, and perhaps even field service will gladly be extended.

For many years now the people who must deal with the vexing problem of unwanted animals have been trying to enlist the help of the public in preventing more and more doomed puppies and kittens from being born. They have made some impression and people are not as heedless as they used to be about letting cats and dogs breed at will and then turning the extra animals out to fend for themselves. But, with cats especially, it is hard to shake the popular notion that a cat on the loose can look after itself. Everyone hates to condemn an animal to death so is tempted to think that it is kinder to abandon it and wish it luck.

Depending on the area and the climate, some of these cats do have luck, just enough luck to get through the winter, hunting and foraging, and in the spring bring up one or two litters. But the process has to stop somewhere and the last stop is unpleasant, both for the cats and the people concerned.

"Your kittens may find a home, but they crowd others into the gas chamber," one of the humane societies points out in a recent plea for help in stemming the tide of overpopulation.

"It is like the game of 'pussy wants a corner.' No matter how homes are shifted about, always there are animals left without a corner. It is the surplus that causes cruelty and suffering. Puppies and kittens are being born at the rate of nearly a quarter-million a day! It is obvious that America cannot provide decent homes for all. The nation's humane societies and pounds are literally drowned in the flood of these animals."

The remedy is as obvious as it is hard to carry out. People simply should not allow kittens to grow up unless they intend to keep them. To accomplish this, most people find that it is preferable to have females spayed rather than undertake the unpleasant job of destroying litter after litter of kittens.

One wishes one could stop here in examining the grimmer side of life for cats today, but unfortunately there is yet another topic that must be included in any conscientious report: the question of the laboratory use of cats, dogs and many other kinds of animals. Cats are not a large proportion of the animals used, yet there are enough of them in laboratories to make their fate of concern to people who love them. Also, I think it is safe to assume that people who are fond of cats or dogs don't stop there but extend their concern to all other animals.

The question of how animals are used in the laboratory has a long history of bitter controversy, accusation and denial, so that the smoke of battle makes it very difficult to find out what it is actually all about. Extremists on both sides, particularly those who have exploited so-called atrocities in the laboratory without hesitating to distort the truth, have so confused and disgusted the public that many people don't want to hear anything about it at all. I confess I wasn't anxious to myself, but I felt that I ought to try and find out whether under all that smoke there was any fire. I've come to the conclusion that there is.

The battle began in England about a hundred years ago. Almost as soon as laboratory science was born, it was obvious that experiments on animals must of necessity involve inflicting considerable pain. In the minds of some people this became a matter of ethical—or even Christian—concern, while to others it seemed of trifling importance as long as the ends justified the means. The first efforts to do something about animal suffering in the laboratory came from two quarters. One was a group dedicated to the total abolition of any scientific use of animals. They called themselves antivivisectionists and continue to fight for that end today. The other group concerned included the most eminent scientists of the day: Huxley, Darwin, Jenner, and prominent members of the medical profession. In 1870 the British Association for the Advancement of Science and the British Medical Association appointed a committee to study "means to reduce to a minimum the suffering entailed by legitimate physiological enquiries; or any which will have the effect of employing the influence of this Association in the discouragement of experiments which are not clearly legitimate on live animals."

A year later the committee reported as follows:

1) No experiment which can be performed under anesthetic ought to be done without it.

2) No painful experiment is justifiable for the mere purpose of illustrating a fact already demonstrated.

3) Whenever, for the investigation of new truth, it is necessary to make a painful experiment, every effort should be made to ensure success, in order that the suffering inflicted

may not be wasted. For this reason, no painful experiment ought to be performed by an unskilled person . . . or in places not suitable to the purpose.

4) Operations ought not to be performed upon living animals for the mere purpose of obtaining greater operative dexterity.

From this report there grew Britain's Act of 1876 which gave to the Home Secretary authority to regulate the use of animals for scientific purposes. The law remains in effect to this day. It provides that experimenters must be licensed, must keep complete records, must have Home Office approval for specific experiments, and must cooperate with government inspectors charged with seeing to it that laboratory animals are in all respects treated as humanely as is practically possible. A proposed experiment that doesn't meet legal criteria can be forbidden by the Home Office. Similar laws are in force in Denmark, Sweden, Switzerland and Belgium.

Even this control did not, however, satisfy the extremists among the anti-vivisectionists who damned it as an unholy compromise. Their agitation has been coupled with such immoderate and abusive attacks on science that scientific leaders who had favored control, and in fact worked to bring it about, became resentful of any lay interference. This is perhaps one of the prime reasons why in the United States today a large number of scientists are not only wary of any mention of the subject, but are inclined in turn to damn as crackpots any group urging legal regulation of laboratory work.

In England the Act of 1876 ended the battle, although the shooting continued. In the United States warfare goes on, and so far the anti-control groups seem to have the upper hand. They have lobbied extensively and successfully against any proposed legislation that would open laboratories to humane workers or government control, and have succeeded in getting new state laws recognizing their right to obtain and use animals without interference.

The problem is not a trivial one. Live animals are vital to the work that goes on in our hospitals, universities and commercial laboratories. Exact figures are unobtainable but undoubtedly many millions of vertebrate animals are used in laboratories yearly. This is not only a colossal number of living creatures, it is a colossal investment in equipment, in food, housing and attendant personnel. It means that a tremendous amount of money is involved. Wherever such huge sums can be affected by legislation, there is bound to be bitter and determined resistance from those currently in charge of spending them. Among the groups dedicated to repelling any invasion of the laboratory by government regulation are the American Medical Association, the Pharmaceutical Manufacturers Association, the National Society for Medical Research and trade organizations representing the laboratory animal industry—those who breed laboratory animals and manufacture equipment.

Ranged against them are, on the one hand, the anti-vivisectionists, and on the other, middle-of-the-road humane groups who do not want to stop the use of animals but do feel that federal regulation like that in Great Britain would prevent unnecessary suffering. These last do not charge that scientists are necessarily willfully cruel, but point out that wherever economics and ethics conflict, as in child labor to give but one example, regulation has been needed to ensure that ethical standards are always met.

The extent of suffering and the necessity for it are, of course, key points in the debate. The moderate group does not claim that all laboratory animals suffer needlessly, but that many do. It charges that some suffering is of the absolute extreme, and can substantiate its charge by quoting from current medical literature. Technical journals do indeed describe procedures that strike the layman as absolutely hair-raising. Those favoring control claim that some of this misery could be abated or avoided. Some painful methods are employed, they say, simply because they are the cheapest and easiest, or because no one has troubled to find another way of accomplishing the same end.

One of the spokesmen for the moderate group urging federal control is the Animal Welfare Institute of New York. It charges that, for reasons of economy, large animals are kept in small cages and remain in them for years, that for the same reason cats, dogs and even monkeys are sometimes kept in extreme discomfort, with nothing to lie on but metal mesh, even after surgery. Student surgeons may practice operations on the same animals over and over, until after six or seven operations the dog or cat is used up. Animals that have been operated on often receive no post-operative care. In some cases experimenters prefer to restrain animals instead of using anesthetics: that is, encase them in a holder or tie them down. Sometimes a drug is used to paralyze the muscles but not the nerves. There is carte blanche in pain infliction so that laboratories answer to no one for the necessity of such violent procedures as rolling animals in drums, breaking teeth and bones, inflicting burns and so on. Experiments may be duplicated needlessly in a number of institutions. Finally, for reasons of economy or simply because of poor administration, the routine handling of animals may be brutal, or they may be starved or infested with vermin.

For several years now, the Animal Welfare Institute and

other groups have proposed legislation, modeled on the British Act of 1876, requiring that all laboratories that use tax funds be licensed and inspected by the federal government. In joining to defeat the bill, the scientific groups reply that such control would hamper their work, cost a great deal of money, increase bureaucratic interference in education and in free enterprise, and in any case is not necessary as they do the best they can to be humane. This rebuttal is, of course, not stated so briefly, but a conscientious search of the arguments turns up very few points that couldn't be thus tidily summed up. Meanwhile the anti-vivisectionists also oppose such legislation on the same ground they have always held: namely, that it doesn't go far enough.

To people who are sensitive about what happens to animals of any kind, the whole subject is a grim one. Furthermore, people mindful of what science has done to diminish human suffering have no wish to interfere with its progress. These two feelings—that the subject is too horrid to think about and that research deserves all possible support—combine to make many people avoid the question entirely.

But surely the matter is not nearly as complicated as the hue and cry make it appear. The need for regulation is clearly as elementary as was the need for child labor laws, or the ordinary laws that prevent cruelty to animals in the community outside the laboratory.

I believe it is possible to serve both science and decency, as has been done in Britain. A British scientist, Professor F. A. E. Crew, F.R.S., commented on the controversy with brilliant simplicity by saying, "I do not think that just anybody should be allowed to do just anything with a living creature." Dr. Albert Schweitzer has written, "What does reverence for life say about the relations between men and the animal world? Whenever I injure any kind of life I must be quite certain that it is necessary. I must never go beyond the un-avoidable."

It is hard to believe that conditions in the laboratories of the United States always meet that standard. It is even harder to see how the doctrine of "never going beyond the unavoid-able" asks too much of anyone, nor how it can be beyond the power and right of our society to enforce.

Chapter XIII

A Thousand Years of Cats

The first cat that came out of the wild to succumb to the blandishments of human beings and the temptations of hearth and larder committed its descendants to the most peculiar destiny of any domesticated species. The story of other animals in domestication is fairly uneventful. On the whole, one would say that dogs have made a fairly good thing of it. Cattle and fowl may not have had particularly

189

enviable lives since they have been regularly eaten, but at least their fate has been orderly and predictable. It has been different with cats. Whether this first cat would have jumped back into the bush if it had foreseen what was in store, no one can tell, but it might at least have thought twice about its fateful act.

If the history of cats is peculiar, it is in no way the fault of the cats. One can assume that they settled down, made themselves as comfortable as possible, and went about their business. People, on the other hand, seldom have been willing to let it go at this. For reasons one can only guess at, cats evoke in humans a gamut of odd responses. Cats have been feared, pampered, encouraged and persecuted. They have been eaten medicinally and admired as objets d'art, worshiped as divine and accused of everything from simple hypocrisy to blackest witchcraft. No other animal has such a record.

The whole body of lore covering the relations between people and cats in the western world can fill many volumes. It has been excellently covered in such books as Agnes Repplier's *Fireside Sphinx*, published in 1901 but still dear to cat connoisseurs, and Carl Van Vechten's *The Tiger in the House*, to name but two of the cat classics. It won't be possible to do more here than sketch in the outlines of the feline's ancient past.

After the close of the cat's Egyptian period, there are hundreds of years of cat history about which almost nothing is known. Cat historians usually ring up the curtain once more on the year 948 A.D. during the reign of a Welsh king named Howel Dda. In this year the good king undertook to revise the law codes of the kingdom. These codes have survived and the articles pertaining to cats make it plain that the Welsh not only kept cats but prized them highly. This in turn allows us to guess that cats were still relatively scarce. Howel Dda's code specified that a newborn kitten was worth one penny; when it opened its eyes, two pennies; when it had killed mice, four pennies. A penny then equaled a lamb or a kid, and four pennies a sheep or a goat. To be worth the full price, the code stated, a cat must be keen of eyesight and hearing, must have "entire" claws, and be willing to rear kittens. Failing any of these, one third the price must be refunded. The code also imposed the difficult provision that "the seller is to answer for her not going caterwauling every moon." The indemnity required of a person who had stolen a cat from the King's granary was a heap of grain equal in height to the length of the cat including its tail. A further suggestion that the measurement be made by suspending the cat by the tail and heaping the grain about it seems as impractical as some of the suggestions of present-day legislators.

Howel Dda's code also stated that a group of dwellings to claim legal status as a hamlet had to possess nine buildings, one plow, one kiln, one churn, one bull, one cock, one herdsman and one cat. In the case of a marital separation, household goods were divided, but the husband got the cat.

While these laws indicate that things were going pretty well for cats, it is nevertheless likely that the cat's fatal association with the occult had already been established, or perhaps had traveled with it from the temples of Egypt.

Just as many a girl has been undone by her good looks, so it seems that most of the woes of the cat can be blamed on its physical attributes. For reasons that go deep into mythology and primitive psychology, men have been both attracted and repelled by the cat's loveliness and have found in it every variety of mystic symbolism. Even today some of these feelings linger on, filtered down to us through the ages. Every school child, in almost every country, is aware that on Halloween cats hobnob with spirits and witches.

Before going into the ways this all worked out for cats, we might take a look at some of the attributes of the cat which have aroused so many eerie ideas.

First, of course, is its sinuosity. Cat haters have called the cat "the furred serpent." The symbolism of the serpent is beyond the scope of a book on cats, but ever since certain unlucky resemblances were noticed, snakes have had a hard time at the hands of man. And cats are tarred with the same brush.

A second unfortunate connection for the cat was with the moon. The moon was once a respectable and powerful pagan deity, but in the long struggle between paganism and the Christian idea of a single, and distinctly male, God, Diana was gradually debased until all that was left to represent her were vile and dangerous witches, of whom the very last is perhaps not dead even yet. There are several things about cats that, in primitive minds, are sufficient to connect them with the moon. First, of course, are their eyes which have such a strange and beautiful luminosity and a seemingly weird ability to penetrate the dark. Men fear the dark and cats do not, which is enough to suggest that the cat has some sort of understanding with whatever power rules the world of night. A she-cat suckling kittens lies in a suggestive crescent and is the very essence of maternity. The moon has often been connected with fertility, amorous passion and the female principle, and all of these are very evident properties of the cat.

The way cats walk noiselessly and leap, as carelessly as though an unseen hand were guiding them, to some high place was enough to put the hair up on many a primitive human. Cats do other things which can be taken as signs that they see, hear and know things imperceptible to human beings. The conformation of the cat's eye gives it a clear yet

192

shallow stare which strikes humans as inscrutable. Its gaze is intense, and yet it is sometimes hard to see just what the cat is looking at, and consequently easy to imagine that it is seeing the unseeable.

Cats have a habit of concentrating when there is apparently nothing to concentrate on, and at other times seem suddenly to respond, with quick attention or an unaccountable leap, to something that isn't there. In other words, they seem to see ghosts. Sometimes a cat's fur crackles with electricity when it is stroked, giving an eerie tingling to the fingers of the stroker, or it may even make tiny visible sparks. This may presage a change in weather, suggesting that the cat had something to do with events in the future. Even the general behavior of cats, so independent of anything but inner dictates, can make it seem as though the cat received guidance from any uncanny source. Sometimes this behavior is connected with a specific event so it appears, by hindsight, that the cat must have been gifted with foresight.

It is easy to see how, in times when everything inexplicable was attributed to occult influence, all these baffling attributes of the cat were enough to damn it as a handmaiden to sinister powers. It is probable, therefore, that from the very beginning of the domestication of cats in Europe, people had ambivalent feelings about them. On the one hand they were valuable and necessary domestic animals. Without cats a farmer dependent on stores of grain would be quite literally eaten out of house and home by rats and mice. Also it is probable that people then were just as capable of fondness for animals as they are now, and cats would have been just as delightful and cozy as pets. But on the other hand cats could, on occasion, bring into the house the dangerous forces of witchcraft against which every man in those days had to be constantly alert.

There were no witches until Christianity arose to give that name to spirits operating outside the church, but the pagan era in Europe was equally hard on cats. A cat flung into a bonfire would have cared little whether it was perishing as a witch or as an embodiment of the corn spirit. The Druids followed the unpleasant custom of burning wicker cages full of live animals as a feature of various ceremonies. The ceremonies survived for hundreds of years after their origin and meaning had been forgotten, in fact survive in paler form until this day. Gradually cats became the most popular victims. Thus for hundreds of years numberless festivals have included the immolation of cats. In early Europe and even later, harvest, spring, Lent, Easter, midsummer or any time of public celebration were all bad times for cats. Even yet, in primitive regions, a cat may be killed as the last bundle of grain is threshed, a memorial to the time when the cat represented the corn god. Until some three hundred years ago, a great midsummer bonfire in Paris annually consumed barrels of cats. In 1648 Louis XIV himself, crowned with a wreath of roses, lighted the fire and danced around it. Earlier in England the coronation of the great Elizabeth included the burning of a huge wicker-work effigy of the Pope, the interior of which was stuffed with squalling cats.

On occasions such as these, cats perished amidst innocent merriment and festivity. In the meantime, with the growth of the church in the Middle Ages, the belief in witches and witchcraft came into flower, bringing a grimmer spirit to the destruction of cats. Witchcraft and the resulting persecution lasted well into the eighteenth century. Sometimes the cat was the witch, or at least a favorite form for a witch to assume; at others it was merely the familiar or partner in crime. It has been reckoned that in the two hundred years of the sixteenth and seventeenth centuries, two hundred thousand witches were executed in Britain and on the continent. The toll in cats must have been heavy indeed.

When brought to justice, witches usually not only confessed their crimes, but incriminated their cats as well, so that early records are filled with proof of the cat's evil ways. The famous Scotch witch, Isobel Gowdie, burned in 1662, confessed that her witch companions prowled in the form of cats, and said that she herself preferred the shape of a hare. One dark night in the year 1566 a group of French farmers ventured into a forest and there surprised an unholy assemblage of cats engaged in mystic rites. The cats attacked them, but the men fought for their lives and managed to escape. In the morning a dozen women of the village were found to bear the wounds of battle and of course confessed the mischief they had done in the form of cats, the night before.

In the Middle Ages animals took part in legal trials even when witchcraft was not concerned. They might be accused or bear witness. Many a cat gave testimony or otherwise influenced the course of justice. At a sixteenth century trial in France, for instance, the attorney for the defense pleaded that his clients, some rats, were unable to appear in court because they feared to cross an intervening stretch of cat territory. The justice and logic of this plea was so irresistible that the rats were acquitted.

From the long years of the cat's incarnation as a witch, a tremendous body of superstitious tales and sayings was born. In various versions they live on in the folklore of every country in Europe. Perhaps most famous is the story of "The King of the Cats." In this, the proverbial midnight traveler encounters a procession of cats carrying a tiny coffin with a crown upon it. Horror-struck, he hurries on and tells his tale at the next village. At this the cottager's cat, which has been drowsing on the hearth, springs up with a weird howl and, exclaiming "Then I am the King of the Cats!" dashes up the chimney in its haste to claim the crown.

Equally familiar in many forms is the tale of the young man whose lovely bride reveals her true nature by leaping from his arms to give chase to a scampering mouse.

In many, many old stories the witch cat gives itself away by speaking with human tongue. The French writer, Champsfleury, tells of a woman who was cooking an omelet when a black cat entered her kitchen. Silently the cat inspected the omelet and then remarked, "It is done. Turn it over!" Outraged at the impudence, the woman threw the omelet at the cat. The next day, of course, she saw a corresponding burn on the face of a neighbor.

Even the common name often given to cats reflected on the company they were supposed to keep. Grimalkin was at first the name of a horrid fiend, but later became a name for any witch's cat, as in the old rhyme:

> Grimalkin, the foul Fiend's cat,
> Grimalkin, the witche's brat.

Rutterkin was a particularly infamous cat; black, with eyes of burning coal, it helped its wicked mistress bewitch the family of the Earl of Rutland so that one by one they sickened and died. Rutterkin's guilt is unfolded in the record of the trial of Joan Flower, convicted as a witch in 1618.

Long after cases of outright sorcery had become rare, more minor superstitions lingered on. Roasting a live cat was considered likely to bring good luck to a house, probably a survival of the earlier notion that if a cat were tortured, the devil, in the shape of a huge cat, would come to its aid and pay a price to redeem it. Likewise all sorts of semimagical medicines and ointments made from various parts of cats were thought helpful in peasant communities for many, many years.

Good or bad luck and the foretelling of the future are the themes of most of the superstitions about cats that remain with us even yet. A cat sneezing on a wedding day brings good luck to the bride. A cat that sits with its tail to the fire knows that it will rain. So, also, does a cat that rubs its paws back of its ears while washing its face. Cats are supposed to scent oncoming death. If a cat should, by any horrid chance, jump over a coffin the most awful consequences may ensue. The usefulness of cats on ships long ago made them regular passengers. Sailors consider calico cats especially lucky and especially good at forecasting foul weather.

And of course the cat has more than its share in wise sayings, proverbs and such.

"A cat with a straw tail sitteth not before the fire."

"He lives under the sign of the cat's foot" is an older way of describing a hen-pecked husband.

"A blind cat makes a proud mouse" is not Russian, but Scottish.

"The cat sees through shut lids" and "Honest as the cat when the meat is out of reach" reflect the widespread belief that cats are less than honorable in their dealings.

Gradually the lot of cats improved, not because cats changed but because people did. Life became gentler and slightly more reasonable. Sensitivity to the feelings not only of other people, but of all other creatures appears more and more frequently in literature and homilies during the eighteenth century. In the English household the cat became an especially beloved pet, to the point where in some places it was a custom for a visitor not only to greet the family and children but to kiss the family cat. Cats, always fascinating playmates to children, became standard nursery pets and it was often pointed out that a cat could teach a child valuable lessons in kindness.

Wholly Cats

I love little pussy,
Her coat is so warm,
And if I don't hurt her,
She'll do me no harm

is a far cry from the earlier attitudes. Other rhymes and stories for the young told of horrid little boys who were cruel to cats and suffered equally cruel retribution. Many prominent people, writers, clergymen, philosophers, and statesmen, were patrons of cats, and the writing of the eighteenth and nineteenth centuries is filled with pleasant and sentimental tributes to them.

These past two hundred years, until quite recently, must have been a golden age for cats almost everywhere. A rural life, barns filled with grain whose attendant mice provided a steady job and a steady diet, roomy kitchens with larders and cellars to be guarded, families that stayed in one place through generations—all of these things made a paradise for cats.

Even the great cities, Rome, London, Paris and New York, had room for cats and work for cats until just a few decades ago. Carriage wheels were not the menace that automobiles are today, and stables provided ideal hunting grounds. Dwellings were still roomy enough, back gardens provided a bit of green, and the inefficiency of street-sweeping departments allowed ample provision for cats with no better place to dine.

Cats made the most of their golden age. That's why there are so many of them today. For those of us who are sentimental it is nice to think that this happy century or two makes up for some of the hard times of the past. But cats are unsentimental and waste no time in historical reflection. Each lives its own life and takes things as they come. Perhaps that is what people mean when they speak of the wisdom of the cat.

Index